THE RETURN OF SHERLOCK HOLMES

The Return of Sherlock Holmes has been novelized from the stage play of the same name by Ernest Dudley (which was itself a very free adaptation of a much earlier [1923] play by Harold Terry and Arthur Rose). Ernest Dudley (the creator of Dr. Morelle) was married to the actress who was a stepdaughter of Ellie Norwood, the famous silent film actor who played Sherlock Holmes on stage many times. Dudley's familiarity with Conan Doyle's famous characters is very evident in this exciting story of blackmail and murder, as Sherlock Holmes pits his wits against his deadly enemy, Colonel Sebastian Moran, second-in-command to Professor Moriarty.

Borgo Press Books by ERNEST DUDLEY

THE RETURN OF SHERLOCK HOLMES

A CLASSIC CRIME TALE

ERNEST DUDLEY

Novelized by Philip Harbottle from the Play

THE BORGO PRESS

MMXII

THE RETURN OF SHERLOCK HOLMES

FIRST EDITION

Published by Wildside Press LLC

www.wildsidebooks.com

DEDICATION

For Susan

CONTENTS

CHAPTER ONE

Cold autumn midday sunshine slanted into a room in Dr. Shlessinger's London nursing home. It was a clinical-looking room, with white walls, centrally located French windows with net curtains, and plain-coloured curtains. It was furnished with a writing desk, table, and chairs. On one side was a door from the hall, and on the opposite wall was a half-open second door that led to the laboratory.

Lady Frances Carfax lay in an easy chair. She was beautiful, but pale. Her eyes were closed, as if asleep. Through the laboratory doorway Cecilia Shlessinger could be seen as she worked in the laboratory. She was attractive in a rather cold way, thirtyish, and wearing a smart nurse's uniform.

Lady Frances suddenly woke up and cried out: "Oh—oh, my God! No—no! Nurse Cecilia!"

At the anguished call Cecilia came hurrying out of laboratory. "All right, Lady Frances...."

"Quickly—quickly!"

Cecilia reached Lady Frances's side. "What is it?"

Lady Frances was now fully awake. "I've had a terrible nightmare. I was being attacked by...."

The nurse took her hand, and sought to calm her. "You're all right now. You're quite safe."

Lady Frances gave a little shudder. "It was a man...a big man...he was dressed like...like...." She shook her head. "He was going to kill me...yet he was smiling and friendly."

"No one is going to kill you," Cecilia soothed.

"But he was! While he was smiling, and he had on this...this black coat...."

The nurse smiled. "It was just a silly nightmare, I tell you. Now, just stay quiet—and I'll bring you your medicine."

"He was a big man—and smiling—"

"Yes, yes. Just you lie quiet." Cecilia hurried back to the laboratory.

Lady Frances called after her: "Is it more of that horrid medicine?"

"No, no. This will be much nicer," the nurse said reassuringly. "I promise you."

"You're sure?" Lady Frances asked doubtfully.

"Quite sure. My brother's made it nicer to taste." The nurse came out of laboratory with a small tray holding a medicine glass, a small jug of water and a medicine phial. She placed them on a table beside Lady Frances, who looked at the tray doubtfully.

The nurse poured medicine into a glass, then after adding a little water, she handed it to Lady Frances.

She took the glass somewhat reluctantly. "Are you sure it's a nicer taste?"

The nurse nodded. "I promise you it is."

Lady Frances drank the medicine and gave a little shudder. "Ugh! It's horrible...horrible!"

She returned the glass to Cecilia, who put it back on the tray, turned, and hurried with it to the laboratory.

Lady Frances took a sweet from her handbag and quickly popped it into her mouth. "Even the sweet doesn't take away the taste. I'm sure this new doctor my brother's got for me won't prescribe such horrid stuff."

Cecilia stood in the laboratory doorway, and stared at Lady Frances with a frozen expression. "No, Lady Frances," she said tightly.

Lady Frances looked up. Instantly the nurse's expression changed. "What did you say his name is...Dr.—Dr Wilson?"

"Watson," Cecilia corrected.

"Dr, Watson...that's right! Well, I hope he'll have something to say about my medicine."

At that moment, a grim-faced man entered from the hall. Dr. Shlessinger was a big man, wearing striped trousers with a black morning coat. As Lady Frances turned to look at him, his expression changed as he quickly adopted a benevolent 'bedside' attitude.

He gave a quick nod to Cecilia, who closed the laboratory door behind her and waited.

He came straight across the room where Lady Frances sat in her easy chair.

"Good morning, Lady Frances," he smiled expansively.

"Oh, Doctor! The medicine's horrible...," Lady Frances complained. "Even worse than before!"

Shlessinger glanced across to Cecilia. "You are serving our patient the correct dose, of course?"

The nurse gave a little shrug. "Yes, I'm following your instructions precisely," she answered formally. Then, with a curt nod to Lady Frances, she crossed the room and went out into the hall.

Shlessinger turned to Lady Frances and looked at her reassuringly. "Now, Lady Frances, you wanted to see me. About...?"

Lady Frances appeared to pull herself together. Reaching for her handbag, she took out a letter from it. She looked up at the doctor.

"Your sister says this came by hand, last night," she said briefly.

Shlessinger nodded. "Yes, that's so," he assented.

Lady Frances glanced down at the letter. She appeared deeply upset. "It's from...from Philip Green. I've tried to read it, but I can't believe what it says. Read it to me, please." She handed letter to Shlessinger.

"I'm sorry it has upset you so much," the doctor murmured, taking the letter.

Lady Frances dabbed at her eyes. "He says he doesn't want to see me again."

"I'm sure he can't mean that."

Lady Frances sniffed. "Read it for yourself."

"If you wish," Shlessinger said, with every appearance of reluctance. He read the letter aloud:

"'My dear: If I have given you cause to believe I cherish feelings for you that are more than friendship'...." He broke off as Lady Frances interjected:

"We were engaged to be married."

Shlessinger paused respectfully for a moment, then continued reading:

"'I am deeply sorry. I feel it better for us both that we should not meet again. Before you receive this, I shall have gone away. Please forgive me. Philip Green'."

Lady Frances began to sob gently.

"I can't believe it, I won't believe it...."

Shlessinger gave her a sympathetic smile. "I'm sure Mr. Green will realize he has made a dreadful mistake and will want to return to you." He handed the letter back to Lady Frances, who agitatedly crumpled it in her hand.

He paused, then added hesitantly: "There is a postscript that I...er...didn't read...."

Lady Frances looked up sharply. "Postscript? What does it say?"

"Really, I...er...." Shlessinger spoke awkwardly. "I think it is only for your eyes, dear lady."

Lady Frances looked down at the letter clutched in her hand and slowly smoothed it out. In a low voice she read: "'As for the bonds, I intend to hang on to them. No one will know where they are'." Tightening her lips, she crushed the letter again and threw it to the floor with a shudder of disgust. Then turned in appeal to Shlessinger.

"You will never mention this to anyone—ever. Please. I forbid you."

"Very well," Shlessinger murmured.

Lady Frances sighed, getting a grip on her emotions. "Now, there's something else," she said hesitatingly. "My brother, I'm afraid, isn't satisfied with my progress."

"I'm very concerned to hear that," Shlessinger said, frowning slightly.

"He was here yesterday, and—"

Shlessinger gave a start. "Lord Henry called here?"

"Yesterday afternoon," Lady Frances affirmed. "And he insisted—"

She broke off as Cecilia entered from the hall.

"Dr. Watson is here, Lady Frances," she announced. "Forgive me for interrupting."

Shlessinger gave a start. "Doctor...Watson? Who...?"

"Lady Frances's new doctor," Cecilia told him calmly.

"I was about to explain," Lady Frances put in.

"Dr. Watson, did you say?" Shlessinger still appeared disconcerted.

"I've taken him to your room," Cecilia told Lady Frances. "He's waiting for you."

"Very well, I'll go along." Cecilia helped her to rise and then escorted Lady Frances out. She looked at her gratefully. "Thank you. Perhaps Dr. Watson will get me well soon, and I'll be able to manage by myself."

Cecilia glanced back over her shoulder and gave Shlessinger a warning look, then turned to Lady Frances and smiled. "I'm sure he will."

Getting Cecilia's message, Shlessinger got a grip on himself. "Yes, of course, I'm sure he will," he called after them.

After they had gone Shlessinger stood in the middle of the room, scowling and muttering to himself. "Dr. Watson? It can't be...."

He broke off as he thought he heard a sound outside the French windows. He started to go across to them, then stopped and shook his head, still muttering to himself. "No, no, it can't be; all the same, something's wrong." Going over to the door, he looked after Cecilia and Lady Frances for a moment, then turned back to the centre of room. "First the damn' brother and now...." He spun and looked to the doorway as Cecilia returned.

"What's been happening?" he demanded. "Who's this Dr. Watson?

"Keep your voice down," Cecilia admonished him.

Shlessinger was still angry. "Not only do you let Lord Henry see her...."

Cecilia spread her hands. "He called out of the blue. I couldn't shut the door in his face, could I?"

Shlessinger calmed slightly. "And now this Dr. Watson—do you realize he must be an imposter?"

Cecilia shook her head.

"No, it's the real one."

"But it can't be," Shlessinger protested. "He hasn't been heard of since Sherlock Holmes's death in Switzerland."

Cecilia remained adamant. "I tell you...." She broke off as the doorbell rang. "That'll be Milverton." She crossed to the door and turned to look back before going on into the hall to admit the caller. "You're expecting him. He'll tell you about Dr. Watson."

Shlessinger exhaled violently. "This is supposed to be a quiet nursing home. It's more like Paddington Station," he muttered, and began pacing up and down, Suddenly he paused, going over to French windows again, and staring out. He failed to see anything, and turned as he heard Cecilia talking to Milverton as she admitted him into the house.

A few moments later Milverton and Cecilia came into the room.

Milverton was a man of about fifty, with a perpetual frozen smile. His keen eyes gleamed brightly behind horn-rimmed glasses. He was wearing a morning suit of perfect cut, and a fur-lined overcoat with collar and cuffs of astrakhan. He was carrying his hat in his hand. He waited, smiling at Shlessinger.

"Mr. Milverton, for Dr. Shlessinger," Cecilia said, formally.

"Good morning, my dear Doctor," the newcomer said affably, his voice smooth and suave. "Charles Augustus Milverton at your service. Charmed to...."

Shlessinger ignored his visitor's extended hand. "All right," he said sourly, "cut the soft soap...save it for your victims."

Cecilia smiled thinly. "I'll leave you two to chat." She turned and went out

"Victims?" Milverton gave an imperturbable smile. "Victims?" he repeated, beaming. "I may be called the greatest scoundrel in London, the mere sound of my name may cause many to blanch, but then, as I try to reassure them, I do you no harm—on the contrary, I protect you against harm, danger, disgrace. So long as you continue to contribute a reasonable sum at intervals convenient to you...."

Shlessinger waved a deprecating hand. "All right. But what's this about Dr Watson?"

Milverton shrugged. "Well, what about him?"

"He's the friend of the late Mr. Sherlock Holmes, who I thought had disappeared without trace. He's here attending our patient."

"You haven't got it quite right," Milverton said quietly.

"It's what Cecilia's just told me," Shlessinger insisted. "I say he's an imposter."

"What I mean is," Milverton explained patiently, "is that Sherlock Holmes is no longer 'the late'; on the contrary, he's very much alive."

"What?" Shlessinger was clearly shocked. "But...but he went over the Reichenbach Falls with Moriarty—"

Milverton nodded. "That's what was *supposed* to have happened. But though Moriarty died, Holmes survived."

"My God...Sherlock Holmes alive." Shlessinger appeared shattered by the news.

"No need to let it worry you," Milverton assured him.

"Worry me? Don't you see what's going on?" He paused to follow Shlessinger's gaze and saw that Cecilia had came back into the room. "So it *is* Dr. Watson," he went on. "Sent to spy on us by Sherlock Holmes."

Seeing her brother's evident agitation, Cecilia glanced at Milverton. "Have you given him the good news?"

"I was coming to that," Milverton said.

Shlessinger looked at him sharply. "Good news?"

"Colonel Moran is taking care of Holmes," Milverton told him complacently.

As realization dawned, Shlessinger gave a grim smile, visibly relaxing. "Moran! Who was Moriarty's closest friend?"

Milverton nodded. "And who is determined to avenge his death."

"So you've nothing to worry about," Cecelia added.

"You can forget Sherlock Holmes," Milverton told Shlessinger. "Lady Frances is all you need concern yourself with."

"But what about her brother?" Shlessinger said, looking at his sister.

The woman shrugged. "He's out of the way now...Zurich... urgent business. He went last night, so...."

"Which brings me to the matter of the letter," Milverton interposed. He took a letter from his inside pocket and handed it to Shlessinger. "Just check that it's the same as the fake her ladyship received."

Shlessinger took letter and began to read bits of it aloud: "'My dear, If I have given you cause to believe...I shall have gone away...please'...." He returned the letter to Milverton. "It's identical," he grunted.

"Postscript and all," Milverton said complacently.

"Postscript and all," Shlessinger agreed.

Milverton pocketed the letter and smiled. "My speciality."

Cecilia looked at their visitor. "Any trouble with her ex-fiancé?" she asked.

"The Colonel's looking after him, all right," Milverton said confidently. He turned to Shlessinger, adding: "Now, to business. I need five minutes with your patient, that's what I'm here for."

Cecilia spread her hands "Dr. Watson's with her at the moment."

"Damn the man!" Shlessinger snapped.

"Look, why not leave her a note?" Cecilia suggested. "Say it's urgent, and that you'll come back this afternoon...."

"Good idea!" Milverton nodded. He went over to the writing desk and, using his fountain pen, began writing on the notepaper he found already on the desk.

"I'll see she gets your note," Cecilia said.

Wolverton looked up. "What time shall I say I'll be here?"

Cecilia thought for a moment. "Say three. I'll fix it."

Milverton finished the letter, placed it into an envelope, and sealed it. He handed it to Cecilia. "I haven't signed it 'Milverton', of course. I've called myself Tamworth...George Tamworth."

Cecilia nodded. "Of course, 'Mr. Tamworth'."

Unseen by the three in the room, a tall figure momentarily flitted past the French window.

"If there's any hitch...," Milverton said, considering, "...if she can't see me...telephone me."

"I'll make sure she sees you," Cecilia assured him.

"There's no time to lose," Shlessinger said.

"Back at three, then." Milverton crossed to the door and went out, followed by Cecilia.

Frowning, Shlessinger looked back and at the French windows and hesitated.

"Come along," Cecilia told him sharply. "We'd better see how Dr. Watson is getting on with our patient."

Shlessinger continued looking at the French windows for a moment, listening intently, then gave a shrug and turned away. "All right, just coming. Thought I heard someone in the garden, but there's no one."

A few moments after they'd left the room, the fleeting tall figure appeared again outside. Suddenly Shlessinger returned, and stood in doorway, looking again at the French windows.

But the figure had gone. Shlessinger waited a moment, then with a shake of his head, turned and went out again. As he did so, the figure reappeared outside.

There came a click of a lock being turned, and Sherlock Holmes entered the room. He was wearing an ordinary suit and hat. Quickly crossing to Lady Frances's chair, he picked up the crumpled letter she had thrown down. He pocketed it and then going quickly to laboratory door, he opened it and entered. A moment later Holmes came out of laboratory with a phial, which he glanced at before slipping it into his pocket. He shut and relocked the laboratory door.

He paused as he heard Lady Frances and Dr. Watson speaking in the hall. Turning back into the centre of room, he took off his hat and awaited their arrival.

Seeing the tall figure of Sherlock Holmes as she entered, Lady Frances gave a violent start.

"Who are you?" she demanded.

"Holmes!" Watson exclaimed as he followed her into the room. "But no one said you were here!"

"That is because I took good care that no one should know."

"This is Mr. Sherlock Holmes," Watson introduced hastily, as Lady Frances continued staring at Holmes, who gave her a little bow.

"How do you do, Lady Frances?" Holmes said, smiling.

Watson glanced at Lady Frances. "As I explained, your brother had a word with Mr. Holmes after his visit here."

"And he seems to think I can be of help to you...over a certain matter," Holmes told her.

Lady Frances frowned at him. "I know I agreed to Dr. Watson's being here, but I didn't think...." She broke off as Shlessinger strode into the room, leaving the door ajar.

"Lady Frances," he began immediately, "I wonder if...." He stopped as he saw Holmes. Instinctively, he pretended not to recognise him. "Who's this? Who are you, sir?"

"My name is Sherlock Holmes, Dr. Shlessinger," Holmes said evenly.

"You have the advantage of me, sir," Shlessinger lied. "But how did you get in here?"

"Mr. Holmes is here at Lord Henry's request," Dr. Watson interposed quickly.

Lady Frances sighed. "I know my brother is interfering, but, since he is my brother, with my welfare at heart...."

Holmes called out, interrupting her: "Do come in, Miss

Shlessinger. You're causing a slight draught, from which I'm sure you wouldn't want your patient to suffer."

Cecilia, who had indeed been listening behind the door her brother had left open, pushed it further open and came into the room.

"Like my brother, I thought you were dea—" She broke off quickly as she saw her brother's glare. "I'm so sorry, please forgive me."

"I fancied a certain Mr. Milverton brought you news that reports of my demise have been grossly exaggerated?" Holmes told her challengingly.

"Milverton?" Shlessinger kept up his pretence. "I don't believe we know anyone of that name."

Holmes raised an eyebrow. "Charles Augustus Milverton?"

Shlessinger looked at his sister. "Can you recall a Mr. Milverton, my dear?"

"Not really...no. Milverton, did you say?"

"Almost the greatest scoundrel in London," Holmes said dryly.

"Of course, we've never heard of such a person," Shlessinger blustered.

Cecilia looked defiantly at Holmes. "I really can't think of anyone."

Holmes smiled cynically. "Yet only a few minutes ago, in this very room, the three of you were discussing a matter of supreme importance. Not only to yourselves, but to Lady Frances."

A nonplussed expression gusted over Shlessinger's face. Then he glanced from Holmes to the French windows and realized it had been Holmes he'd heard outside. He continued to try and bluff his way out. "What are you saying?" He turned to Watson. "Really, Dr. Watson, your friend...."

Lady Frances looked at Shlessinger fixedly. "Is this true?" she demanded.. "That you were discussing me with Mr.—Mr.—?"

"I assure you that Mr. Holmes is imagining things," Shlessinger said.

Lady Frances swung her gaze back to Holmes. "You seem

to know something which I don't! What has my brother been telling you?"

"He believes you to be in some danger....," Holmes told her.

Shlessinger bridled. "Danger? What nonsense! Why—" he stopped as Cecilia tugged at his arm.

Lady Frances turned to Dr. Watson. "But I'm not really ill, you said."

"Dear Lady Frances," Cecilia said insinuatingly, "I'm so sorry you're being distressed in this way."

Lady Frances wavered. "What should I do, Dr. Watson?" she appealed to him.

Watson spoke firmly. "Perhaps you should listen to what Mr. Holmes has to say."

Lady Frances looked again at Cecilia, then Shlessinger, who glanced at Cecilia. His sister gave a little shrug.

"No doubt Mr. Holmes is anxious to earn the fat fee he's been paid," she said. "I suggest that we allow him to try his best." She signalled to her brother: "Come along, my dear."

"Very well." Shlessinger spoke reluctantly. He looked coldly at Holmes. "Perhaps you'll be good enough to let us know when you're ready to leave."

Lady Frances turned to Watson as he brought forth a chair and invited her to sit down.

Cecilia smiled at her sympathetically and turned to leave, followed by Shlessinger.

"A moment, Miss Shlessinger," Holmes said sharply. The Shlessingers stopped and turned to him. Holmes extended his right hand. "The letter, please. May I see it?"

They glanced at each other, then at Holmes, as if mystified.

"Letter? What letter?" Shlessinger blustered.

"Letter, Mr. Holmes?" Cecilia frowned.

Holmes crossed to her, continuing to hold his hand extended.

Cecilia gave him a frozen smile.

"If you please?" Holmes said firmly.

Cecilia affected to suddenly realize to what Holmes had been referring to. "Oh, *that* letter."

Shlessinger became alarmed. "What is it? Some prescription or something? Give it here." He held out his hand.

"Isn't it addressed to Lady Frances?" Holmes said sharply. Cecilia hesitated momentarily, then shrugged and gave the letter to Lady Frances.

She started to open it, then handed it to Dr. Watson. "You read it for me, Dr. Watson, please."

Watson glanced at Holmes, who gave a nod. He took the letter and opened it. After a quick scan, he summarized its contents:

"It is from a Mr. Tamworth, requesting an appointment. He says it's something very confidential about which he can help you."

Lady Frances frowned, "But who is Mr. Tamworth? I don't know anyone of that name."

"Perhaps I may explain," Holmes interposed crisply. "'Tamworth' is an alias adopted by the aforementioned Mr. Milverton, who happens to be a notorious blackmailer!"

Lady Frances looked aghast. "A blackmailer?" she whispered.

Holmes continued his revelations. "Criminals when choosing an alias, invariably pick a name which has some connection with the crime they are planning." He paused, and then addressed a question to Shlessinger, who, with Cecilia, had been pretending to look shocked. "What is this address, by the way?"

"Address? Address...." Shlessinger looked at his sister. "What does he mean?"

"It's the Laurels Nursing Home, *Tamworth* Road, of course." Watson pointed out dryly.

Holmes nodded. "You see, Mr. Milverton runs true to form in his choice of another name."

"But what am I to do?" Lady Frances faltered.

Shlessinger attempted a bluff. "I think we should fetch the police—" he glared at Holmes—"unless you leave at once."

Lady Frances became alarmed. "Police! No, no, that's the last thing you must do."

Holmes smiled sardonically. "Believe me, Lady Frances, it is the last thing *he* will do."

"Don't be too sure of that," Shlessinger snapped. He turned to his sister. "Come along, my dear, we...we must consult our solicitors about this matter." He took her arm.

Cecilia allowed herself to be led from the room. "Yes, yes, of course, our solicitors...."

"Sue for slander, that's what we'll do...," Shlessinger muttered as they went out.

Holmes moved over to where Lady Frances was sitting dazedly on the chair Watson had provided.

"Now, Lady Frances, I'd like to look at your hands." He glanced at Watson who was hovering solicitously at her side. "Dr. Watson?"

Watson nodded as Lady Frances looked at him. "Mr. Holmes is an authority on poisons."

"Poisons?" She extended her hands quickly.

Holmes examined them carefully.

"The medicine you took a short while ago...," he murmured, raising an interrogative eyebrow,

"Which Nurse Shlessinger gave me?" Lady Frances asked, her voice wavering.

Holmes nodded. "It made you feel cold?"

"Yes, very cold...deathly...as I told Dr. Watson...."

"I've changed the prescription, of course." Watson said promptly.

"And rather dizzy?" Holmes continued, releasing her hands.

"Yes. I couldn't think properly."

"What you have been taking," Holmes explained, "was administered to you for the precise purpose of weakening your willpower, preparatory for an attempt at blackmail."

Lady Frances stared at him in disbelief. "Blackmail? Oh, my God!" She swung to Watson. "Is...is this true?"

"I'm afraid so."

"You have been the victim of a deliberate plot," Holmes told her. "But fortunately, your brother suspected, and came to Watson."

"You mean, Dr....Dr. Shlessinger and his sister...?" Lady Frances whispered.

"...are notorious criminals, who intend to bleed you of every penny you possess!" Holmes finished bluntly.

"Oh!" Lady Frances slumped in her chair.

Watson took her hands comfortingly. "You are safe now. Absolutely out of danger."

"What...what had the man with the two names got to do with all this?" Lady Frances asked.

"I will explain everything later," Holmes assured her. His tone became urgent. "But now, we must get you away from here."

"But where shall I go?"

"An hotel, where your brother has arranged for you to stay," Holmes told her. "You can stay there until all this has blown over." He pointed to the French windows. "Dr. Watson will see you safely by way of the garden. I've got a cab waiting." He glanced at his watch. "It's all according to plan."

Watson and Lady Frances followed Holmes to the French windows.

He was just opening the windows for them when Shlessinger and Cecilia came into the room. Shlessinger strode forward angrily.

"What the devil's going on?"

"They're kidnapping our patient," Cecilia commented.

Holmes ushered Watson and Lady Frances out into the garden. "Hurry, hurry...."

When they had gone he closed the windows and turned calmly back into the room.

"Damn your eyes!" Shlessinger snarled.

Holmes tapped his pocket where he'd put the phial taken from laboratory. "I've got here the poison you were giving to Lady Frances. "Evidence to jail you both."

"The phial! He's got the phial!" Cecilia screeched furiously.

Cecilia following, Shlessinger lunged forward, his hands extended. "You can't think you'll get away with this!"

They halted in their tracks as Holmes suddenly produced a small revolver from his other pocket. "Put your hands up!" he snapped.

Shlessinger started to obey, but Cecilia resumed moving forward.

"It's only a toy!" she cried. "He's bluffing! Stop him!"

Shlessinger moved towards Holmes, only to halt abruptly as the detective fired a shot at his feet.

"My God!" Shlessinger shouted. "He'll kill us!"

"I shan't warn you again," Holmes said evenly. "Hands up and keep them up!"

This time both Shlessinger and his sister obeyed. Keeping them covered and forcing them back, Holmes crossed quickly to the open door. Still keeping them covered, he took out the key from it with his free hand. At that moment a loud taxi-hoot sounded from the street.

"Just coming!" Holmes murmured, darting out and slamming door after him.

Shlessinger and Cecilia rushed towards the door, then halted as they heard the key turning in the lock.

Shlessinger began wrenching at the door handle. "He's locked us in! You'll pay for this, Holmes!" he shouted.

"Yes!" Cecilia screeched in rage. "Colonel Moran will see to that. D'you hear, Mr. Bloody Sherlock Holmes? Moran'll settle your hash!"

She quivered with rage as another taxi-hoot sounded outside.

CHAPTER TWO

It was late in the afternoon on the same day as Sherlock Holmes and Dr. Watson had contrived the rescue of Lady Frances Carfax from Shlessinger's Nursing Home. Holmes had just finished tea in his comfortable room on the first floor at his Baker Street home. He pushed back his chair and lighted his pipe, looking about him.

A telephone projected from the wall beside the door leading to the landing outside it. A warm fire crackled in the fireplace against the back wall. From the coal scuttle protruded a box of cigars, a Persian slipper serving for a tobacco jar. Holmes' reflective gaze travelled to the window, overlooking Baker Street, then along the bookshelves lining the far wall. In front of them was a writing desk littered with papers, pipes, and odds and ends, on which had been thrown a violin and bow. On either side of the desk were two shabby but comfortable armchairs. A mass of correspondence for attention was pinned to a bookshelf by a jackknife.

Footsteps sounded from the landing outside, followed by a gentle but firm knock on the door.

"Come in," Holmes called. His housekeeper entered, carrying a tray. "Thank you, Mrs. Hudson," he added, as the woman deftly placed his tea-things on the tray.

Just as she turned to go out, the front door bell rang. Holmes glanced at his watch and frowned slightly.

"Now, who could that be?" Mrs. Hudson said. She left to answer the summons, taking the tray with her.

"Dr. Watson's probably forgotten his key," Holmes murmured as she went out.

"Not like him to do that," Mrs. Hudson commented over her shoulder. Still carrying the tray as she went downstairs she called out, "All right, Doctor, I'm coming."

Holmes put down his pipe and crossed to the writing desk, where he picked up his violin. Downstairs, after setting aside her tray, Mrs. Hudson opened the front door.

"Inspector Lestrade?" she exclaimed in surprise. "I thought it was...."

"Afternoon, Mrs. H.," Lestrade greeted her in his brisk cockney accent, full of self-importance. "And how are you?"

Hearing the exchange through his open door, Holmes put down his violin and returned to the table, his manner alert. "Lestrade?" he muttered to himself. "What can he want?"

Mrs. Hudson called up the stairs. "It's Inspector Lestrade, Mr. Holmes."

"Lestrade of the Yard," he called after her.

Mrs. Hudson regarded him quizzically. "You usually gives three short, sharp rings, Inspector."

"Ah, that's when I'm expected, Mrs. H.," Lestrade smiled. "I wasn't this time, you see."

He looked up as Holmes's voice sounded from the top of the stairs.

"Come on up, Inspector."

Lestrade lost no time in hurrying upstairs, and into Holmes' room.

"Good afternoon, Mr. Holmes." Lestrade had come in plain clothes, and was wearing a dark overcoat. Putting his bowler hat on the table, he shook hands with Holmes.

"Good afternoon, Inspector. This is an unexpected pleasure."

"I'll get down to business straight away," the Inspector said. "It's to do with Colonel Moran."

Holmes raised an eyebrow. "Moran?"

"He's in London," Lestrade said urgently.

"Is he now?"

"And seeing as how his purpose in being here concerns you directly, I thought you should know."

"Many thanks, indeed."

"My information," Lestrade went on, "is that he's got that special gun of his with him." He looked at Holmes grimly.

"The walking-stick gun?"

"The very same what blew young Ronald Adair's head clean off his shoulders." Lestrade gave a shudder. "Made even me—who's seen a few nasty sights in his time—feel sick in the stomach."

Holmes nodded gravely. "It's a murderous weapon, I agree."

"And I'm sure I don't have to tell you who he plans to aim it at this time. He's obsessed that you killed his pal, Moriarty."

"You have my full attention, Inspector," Holmes told him.

"I'm here to warn you to find yourself a quiet little country pub and lie low until I give you the tip-off that I've got Moran safely behind bars." Lestrade's tone indicated his confidence in his own ability to bring the notorious criminal to book.

Holmes was unconvinced. "But on what charge? You weren't able to nab him over the Adair case, though both you and I knew he was as guilty as hell."

"He's behind a blackmail plot—not his normal line of business—but he's using it to mask his real aim, which is *you*."

"The blackmail plot you refer to concerning the Shlessinger brother and sister?" Holmes asked, and Lestrade frowned.

"The same. You know about them?" he asked sharply.

"As it happens, I do."

"Involving 'Gussie' Milverton...Charles Augustus of that ilk?"

Holmes nodded. "The same."

Lestrade hesitated. "Look, Mr. Holmes," he said, slowly. "I won't ask no more questions. I wouldn't get answers if you didn't want to give them, anyway. You're a private detective, with your client to think of, but I tell you, I mean to get Moran on a blackmail charge and see him put away in Dartmoor for twenty years. Which will put you out of danger for a long time."

"An exercise on which, you may rest assured, I will be only too happy to cooperate," Holmes told him.

Lestrade appeared mollified. "Many thanks, Mr. Holmes. We'll keep in touch, then."

They shook hands and Lestrade turned to the door. "And remember me to Dr. Watson."

"I will, of course," Holmes murmured.

Just then came the sound of the front door downstairs opening, and the voices of Mrs. Hudson and Dr. Watson drifted up the stairs.

"It's I, Watson," the doctor called as he ascended the stairs. "Bit late, I'm afraid, only...." He broke off as he encountered Lestrade in the doorway. "Oh, hello, Inspector."

"Afternoon, Doctor," Lestrade acknowledged. "And how are you, then?"

"Very well, thank you."

Lestrade grinned. "But, of course, you needs to be, don't you? Your stock in trade, to be 'ale and 'earty. Otherwise your patients would take their pains elsewhere." He gave a chuckle. "So long, Doctor. Bye, Mr. Holmes." He began to descend the stairs. "Afternoon, Mrs. H. I'll see meself out."

"Afternoon, Inspector." The housekeeper said. "Goodbye."

Upstairs Holmes and Watson heard the front door open and close. Watson closed the door to Holmes' room and looked anxiously at his friend.

"What is it, Watson?"

"I'm rather concerned. Lady Frances isn't at her hotel...."

Holmes appeared unworried. "I know. I have made other temporary arrangements."

"Oh! Is that why Lestrade was here?"

"No, no, entirely another matter. I've enrolled Lady Frances's help in another plan I'm putting into effect."

Watson relaxed somewhat. "Well, I'm thankful she's all right." He came into the room and sat in his usual armchair.

Holmes regarded him steadily. "Now, listen carefully. Colonel Moran has made his first move." He indicated the window.

Watson glanced uneasily at the window. "What's he up to?"

"He's rented a room in the house opposite."

Watson gave a start. "Rented a room?"

Holmes nodded. "On the third floor...it commands a good view."

Watson frowned. "Of...of this room?"

"Precisely."

"Was that what Lestrade came to warn you about?" Watson asked.

Holmes nodded. "Though I already knew. I'd learned it from my own observation...and certain enquiries that I made."

Watson looked uneasily at the window as realization dawned. "So you'll be in his line of fire? And he'll have that dreadful gun of his."

"That is what Lestrade came to warn me about," Holmes affirmed. "Moran means to exact his revenge for my killing his companion in crime, Moriarty."

Watson tightened his lips. "When really it was Moriarty who tried to kill *you*."

Holmes spread his hands. "Whatever—but Moran means to extract his revenge."

"And you're going to give him the chance," Watson said accusingly.

Holmes shrugged. "We shall see.... What Lestrade did tell me is that Moran is behind the Shlessingers' scheme to blackmail Lady Frances."

Watson looked surprised. "You mean he's using that in order to reach you?"

"That is what it amounts to," Holmes assented. Then he glanced at the door as there came the sound of the front door bell ringing again.

"That'll be Lady Frances, I expect." Watson said. "Don't you think, Holmes, she is singularly appealing?"

Holmes smiled faintly. "I consider her case singularly appealing; especially now that Moran's involved."

Downstairs, Mrs. Hudson was opening front door. Watson's

surmise about the latest visitor had been incorrect.

"Good afternoon, madam," Milverton said. "I believe I'm expected."

"You're to go on up, sir." Mrs, Hudson told him.

"Thank you, my dear," Milverton murmured smoothly, moving towards the stairs.

"It's the gentleman, Mr. Holmes," Mrs. Hudson called up behind him.

Watson, for once, was completely taken aback. He stared blankly at Holmes as Milverton entered.

Milverton insinuated himself into the room, leaving the door open a few inches behind him.

The visitor was wearing the same suit and overcoat as he had at the Nursing Home. He stretched out his hand to shake hands with Holmes as Watson stared disbelievingly.

"Mr. Sherlock Holmes...delighted to meet you," Milverton murmured suavely.

Holmes ignored Milverton's hand. "Good afternoon," he said briefly. He nodded to his friend. "Dr. Watson."

"Ah, yes, of course." Milverton extended a hand to Watson who also pointedly ignored it. Milverton's smile remained intact. "How d'you do, Doctor?"

"Good afternoon," Watson said coldly.

"This is Mr. Milverton," Holmes said.

"Charles Augustus Milverton," The visitor said smugly. "Charmed, I'm sure."

Watson was still staring at Holmes, waiting for an explanation.

Holmes gave it. "Whom I've persuaded to call to discuss a matter in which we share an interest."

"Just a quiet business chat," Milverton murmured.

Holmes reached into his pocket and took out a letter, which he began reading. "'Dear Lady Frances Carfax.... I am in possession of some information concerning yourself and the Honourable Philip Green, about which I can be of help to you. It is of some urgency, so will call this afternoon at three o'clock in

the hope you will see me. Yours sincerely, George Tamworth'."
He glanced at Watson and added dryly: "Mr. Milverton sometimes prefers to be known by an alias."

Milverton shrugged. "One's business practice often calls for
discretion."

Holmes regarded him steadily. "And what was this information, which was a matter of such urgency?"

"Lady Frances," Milverton explained, "was engaged to be
married to the Honourable Philip Green, a member of the distin-
guished firm of solicitors, of which her brother, Lord Cecil,
is the head. Green, however, had met and fallen in love with
Cecilia Shlessinger, who at the time was nursing Lady Frances."

"Nursing!" Watson burst out scornfully. "She and her brother
were systematically poisoning her, as part of a blackmail plot."

"My dear sir," Milverton smiled, "there is nothing you can
tell me about the Shlessingers I haven't made it my business
to find out. It's their speciality...persuading unsuspecting rich
women that they can be cured of some imaginary illness." He
reached into his own pocket and took out a letter, which he
handed to Holmes.

Holmes gave Milverton a grim look and began to read the
letter aloud: "'My dear.... If I have given you reason to believe I
cherish feelings for you that are more than friendship, I am duly
sorry. I feel it is better for us both, if we don't meet again....' He
broke off. "I have already read this, of course."

"Including the postscript?" Milverton pressed.

Holmes looked at the letter again. "'As for the bonds, I intend
to hang on to them. No one will know where they are'." He
looked at Milverton. "How did you come by this?"

"It was given to me."

"By whom?" Holmes asked sharply.

Milverton pointed to the letter in Holmes' hand. "Him."

"Knowing what use you intend to make of it?"

Milverton nodded. "He wanted £250 for it. We settled for
£100."

"So Philip Green is party to your scheme to blackmail his

ex-fiancée?" Holmes asked thoughtfully.

Milverton nodded. "He'd already absconded with her bonds, so why not pick up a little extra while he was about it?"

Holmes looked at the frowning Watson. "It makes one wonder, doesn't it, how Lady Frances could have been in love with such a rogue in the first place."

Watson shook his head. "It does indeed, Holmes."

"Some women prefer rogues," Milverton smirked. "So I'm told."

Holmes looked again at the letter. "I notice it says: 'I have gone away'. And, no doubt, he left no forwarding address."

Milverton shrugged. "I wasn't sufficiently interested to ask."

"Of course," Watson said acidly, "your only interest is the saving of Lady Frances's reputation?"

Milverton smiled. "And her brother's, don't forget. Imagine the damage to Lord Cecil's reputation...not to mention his standing in Society...if it became known that a member of his firm had, shall we say, jilted his sister and absconded with the loot."

"And what," Holmes asked pointedly, "is the asking price to prevent what you have so graphically described?"

"A mere ten thousand."

"You scoundrel!" Watson shouted.

Holmes waved a deprecating hand. To Milverton he said: "In exchange for your copy...the only existing copy...of this letter?" He indicated Green's first letter.

"That is the deal," Milverton affirmed.

"Would you, as part of the...er...'deal', rack your brains and contrive to recall where Philip Green might be?" Holmes asked pointedly.

Milverton stared at him. "I can't," he said slowly. "I tell you, I don't know."

"You disappoint me." Holmes murmured. "But let us suppose my client, however reluctantly, agrees to your demand, how can you be trusted not to retain another copy of the letter?"

Milverton spread his hands and smiled. "You must accept

my word,"

"The word of a blackmailer!" Dr. Watson snapped angrily.

Holmes smiled enigmatically. "Tell me, Mr. Milverton, how would you describe yourself? As a brave man, or a rather timid one?"

Milverton looked surprised. "I...I would describe myself simply as a reasonable person, inclined to generosity," he said slowly.

Holmes turned and crossed to his writing desk, with his back to Milverton. He began to open a drawer in the desk. "You see, you—a known criminal—came here, unaccompanied...."

"At your invitation," Milverton said.

Still fiddling with the desk drawer, Holmes continued speaking slowly: "With the object of extracting from Lady Frances Carfax £10,000 in exchange for a letter written to her by an acknowledged accomplice. Surely, then, all I need do by way of reply...." Taking a revolver from desk drawer, Holmes suddenly spun round, and aimed it at Milverton. "...is shoot you down like the dog you are!"

Watson gave a gasp of astonishment. "Holmes!"

Holmes smiled grimly as Milverton cringed. "With Dr. Watson here as witness that when, on behalf of my client, I refused your demand, you attacked me...which, of course, I will explain to Scotland Yard."

"And I'll back you up, every word!" Watson vowed.

Milverton was badly scared. "If...if you did that, my death would be avenged," he said, rallying. "You would be dead within twenty-four hours."

"I see...so you have accomplices, other than Green?"

Milverton remained silent for a while, realizing he had said to much. Then: "We're talking about you and me...when it's your client we should be discussing...her future happiness and peace of mind which are at stake."

Deadlock. Holmes stared intently at Milverton, who returned the stare, before eventually glancing away. At length Holmes gave a shrug.

"A very persuasive argument." He returned his revolver to the writing desk drawer, then turned back to Milverton. "Very well, I will let you have Lady Frances's decision as soon as possible."

Milverton relaxed a little. "If you would telephone me tomorrow—you have my number?"

"Yes...I have your number."

"Say at midday?" At Holmes' nod, Milverton continued: "And we can arrange a meeting when the transaction can take place, to our mutual satisfaction."

"You will bring the only other copy of this...." Holmes placed the first letter with the second letter on the table.

"And you will have the cash," Milverton said flatly.

Holmes nodded. "If that is my client's wish." He looked at Watson. "Will you see Mr. Milverton finds a cab?"

Watson frowned. "A cab? Oh, all right."

"Good afternoon, Mr. Milverton," Holmes said heavily.

"Good afternoon, sir...charmed to have made your acquaintance." Milverton went out, followed by Watson.

After waiting until he heard the two men talking to Mrs. Hudson downstairs, Holmes called out quietly:

"All right. My Lady, you may come out of hiding."

Lady Frances Carfax emerged from a cupboard. She was dressed in smart. everyday clothes, and was struggling to keep her emotions under control.

"You were marvellous, Mr. Holmes." she told him.

At that moment Dr. Watson came back into the room, and froze in astonishment. "Lady Frances! But where have you sprung from?"

Holmes smiled faintly. "My client and I agreed it would be a good idea for her to know precisely—word for word, in fact, every detail of this attempt to blackmail her."

Watson came forward and arranged a chair for Lady Frances, but she elected to remain standing. "You are very brave," he commented.

Lady Frances tossed her head. "And, of course, it is all lies... horrible lies. Philip's not a thief...he's not!"

"Of course not," Holmes assented. "Milverton gave us proof of that." He indicated the two letters he had placed on the table.

"How do you mean?" Lady Frances asked.

"That was one reason for my asking him here," Holmes explained. "As I surmised, the letter Philip Green is supposed to have written to you is a forgery."

Lady Frances clenched her fists. "Oh, my God...that dreadful man!"

"How can you tell that?" Watson asked.

Holmes held out both letters for the others to see. "Compare the 'S' in Milverton's 'Dear Lady Frances', it's remarkably similar to the 'S' in 'sorry' in Green's letter."

Watson and Lady Frances stared at the letters, then nodded their heads in agreement.

"Note the 'R' in 'cherish' and 'friendship' is identical with the 'R' in 'information' and 'afternoon' in this." Holmes went on, indicating the second letter. "The only differences in the handwriting is that the letter supposed to be from Philip Green was written with an ordinary pen, Milverton's with a fountain pen."

"He didn't foresee you would read both letters." Watson pointed out.

Holmes nodded. "Even the shrewdest of us can't foresee every eventuality."

"If Philip didn't write that...that letter, where is he?" Lady Frances faltered.

"I'm afraid that he's held captive," Holmes told her gently.

"A prisoner?" Watson regarded Holmes anxiously. "Who's holding him?"

Lady Frances put her hand to her head and sank into the chair.

Quickly Holmes waved a hand to Watson indicating that he should say nothing more, and turned to the distraught Lady Frances. She looked up at him imploringly.

"But he's alive...they haven't...?"

"I'm sure he is in no danger," Holmes said reassuringly.

"His captors could have no reason to harm him," Watson added quickly.

"So long as that creature gets his money," Lady Frances said miserably.

"No, no...." Holmes shook his head. "He won't." He leaned down and took hold of Lady Frances's arm. "Now, you can rest assured that the man you love and who loves you is not the scoundrel he was made out to be."

"I...I never really thought he could be," she said quietly.

"Now, I want you to return to your hotel," Holmes said crisply, helping her to get to her feet. "A cab is waiting for you," he added, glancing at his watch.

"I'm so grateful to you," she said, releasing his hand.

"I want you to wait there," Holmes instructed her, "until Dr. Watson and I bring Philip Green to you, to tell you, in person, that he's safe."

"I will see you safely back," Watson said promptly.

"No, Watson," Holmes cut in. "Mrs. Hudson will accompany Lady Frances."

"Oh!" Watson looked his disappointment.

"Thank you, Mr. Holmes." Lady Frances turned to go, then noticed Holmes's violin on the writing desk. "A violin!" She picked it up carefully. "Do you play?"

"Occasionally, when I have time...."

"Oh, how wonderful," Lady Frances enthused. "I adore the violin. You must come to my next musical evening. I used to have them regularly and, now I'm better, I shall start again."

"You're very kind," Holmes demurred, "but really I play only for my own amusement...."

"Nonsense, Holmes!" Watson said. "I think you play very well."

Holmes moved quickly to door and called downstairs to his landlady. "Mrs. Hudson! Lady Frances is just leaving."

"Yes, Mr. Holmes," she called back. "The cab is ready, waiting."

"Thank you, Mrs. Hudson," Holmes called back. Then he

turned to lady Frances. "When you're ready."

"I'll see you downstairs," Watson said eagerly.

Lady Frances smiled, "Thank you, Doctor."

Holmes stayed at door as they hurried downstairs. Suddenly the wall telephone began ringing, and Holmes glanced at his watch. Slowly he went to the telephone, and paused. The phone stopped ringing. Holmes waited. Then the phone started ringing again, After waiting for a few moments, Holmes lifted the phone.

"That you, Billy? Right on time...what's your news? Oh, did he? So instead, you dropped him at the corner, I see. Splendid. I will be in touch with your well-earned fee." Smiling to himself, Holmes hung up.

He turned as Watson re-entered the room.

"I heard you on the telephone as I came up the stairs," he said. "Who's Billy?"

"My taxi-driver spy...who took Milverton back to where he lives."

"Ah, yes, of course," Watson said admiringly. "You always did have the best underworld contacts...as you call them...in London."

"London?" Holmes raised an eyebrow, "My dear Watson, I have access to the most comprehensive 'grapevine'...to use the vernacular...in all Europe."

"Yes...yes...," Watson said hurriedly. "And what did he report?"

"Milverton, as I rather suspected he might, switched the address he first gave to the corner of Tamworth Road, and walked...."

"...To the Shlessingers' Nursing Home?" Watson asked shrewdly.

Holmes nodded. "And the hairs at the back of my neck—are prickling, Watson."

"You mean?"

"Moran is using the Shlessingers' attempts at blackmailing Lady Frances to lure me to my destruction...correct?"

"I suppose so," Watson admitted worriedly, "but how?"

"In his Indian Army days the Colonel's hobby was big game hunting, at which he was renowned. His *modus operandi* was to tie a young goat to a tree in the vicinity where he knows his quarry hunts his prey, while he waits hidden with gun...." Holmes tightened his lips. "That very special gun of his...ready for the kill."

Watson gave a little shiver. "And in this case?"

"Philip Green is the prey; I am the quarry."

Abruptly the phone rang again. Watson started, then smiled apologetically at Holmes, who was making no move to answer the phone.

"Another of your underworld contacts?"

"If you would be kind enough to answer it...," Holmes told him.

"Of course." Watson hurried to the phone, and was about to answer it, when he turned to Holmes. "Are you at home?"

Holmes shrugged.

Watson put his hand over the mouthpiece as he listened to the voice at the other end of phone. "It's that so-called nurse, putting on a voice, asking for me."

Holmes strode forward quickly and taking the phone from Watson, said:

"This is Sherlock Holmes speaking...who is that?" Cecilia's voice sounded indistinctly. "No...Dr. Watson's left to visit a patient." He paused; there was no reply

Holmes hung up.

"It *was* her, wasn't it?" Watson asked. "Why would she want to speak to me?"

Holmes shrugged and smiled faintly. "She didn't. It was a device to find out if I am alone." He turned to look across at the window.

Watson followed his glance. "For Colonel Moran's benefit, of course." As Holmes nodded, he added: "And now he believes you are alone...?"

"...Doubtless, he will act."

Watson watched nervously as Holmes went to the mantel-piece, taking his pipe from his pocket. He filled it from the Persian slipper, taking his time.

Watson shifted his gaze from Holmes to the window, and back again. He watched as Holmes lit up, and puffed at his pipe, blowing smoke towards the window.

Holmes held out his free hand towards Watson. "Your hat, Watson," he requested.

Watson frowned, not understanding the reason for the odd request. As Holmes snapped his fingers impatiently, Watson picked up his hat from where he'd placed it on the back of a chair, and handed it to Holmes.

The detective took a deep drag at his pipe, and as he expelled tobacco-smoke towards the window, he suddenly threw his hat up, also towards the window.

Instantly a pane of glass in the window was shattered by a bullet that smashed into a large vase on the mantelpiece, causing it to crash in several pieces into the fireplace with a startling effect.

"My God!" Watson jumped as if he had been shot.

The bullet lodged in a large book on the mantelpiece, knocking it down into the fireplace. It brought down other books after it, adding to the terror of the shot.

"All right," Holmes said coolly. "No harm done."

As Watson started to go to window, Holmes halted him.

"Stay where you are, Watson," he warned. "You're not here, remember...you're visiting a patient."

Watson was visibly shaken. "Yes, yes, of course," he gasped.

Holmes stooped down to pick the bullet out of the book. "A rifle bullet designed to explode on impact, inflicting extensive damage," he murmured, examining it.

"But this is attempted murder. Horrible murder!" Watson said.

Holmes nodded calmly. "My hope is that Moran feels he's succeeded in his attempt."

"I...I don't follow," Watson said dazedly.

"He believes me to be alone," Holmes explained crisply, "so his next step must be to send someone to ascertain if the bullet has found its billet."

He crossed to the writing desk, opened a drawer, and took out a mask of a shattered, blood-stained face. He placed the mask over his own face, and turned to Watson.

The effect was quite horrific.

"As a doctor, how's this for a human face shattered by that bullet?" he asked sardonically.

"Very realistic." Watson turned away with a little shudder.

Holmes smiled behind the hideous mask. "Splendid! Now, I predict, they'll be over any second to check the damage."

Even as he finished speaking the front door bell rang downstairs.

Watson was flustered. "But who'll let them in? Mrs. Hudson's out."

"Of course," Holmes murmured. "That's why I sent her off with Lady Frances."

Watson stared incredulously at Holmes. "You mean—you've *planned* all this?"

Holmes handed Watson his revolver, and pushed him towards his bedroom. "They'll have a skeleton key."

As Watson closed the bedroom door behind him, Holmes quickly sprawled on floor.

Downstairs the front door opened and there came the sound of footsteps ascending stairs rapidly.

Holmes groaned loudly, as if in agony.

Cecilia's voice sounded outside the door. "Is anyone there?"

Holmes groaned again. The door opened.

"Mr. Holmes?" Slowly Cecilia entered the room.

"Help me," Holmes groaned feebly, "Help me...."

Cecilia went across to Holmes, and stared down at him with simulated horror. "Oh, my God, who' done this?"

"Milverton...," Holmes gasped.

"Milverton?"

"I...I've put a stop to his blackmail..." Holmes coughed thickly and groaned again. "Get help quickly...or I'm done for."

Cecilia straightened and turned for the door. "I'll find help, trust me! She went out, calling back. Quick as I can...."

As she went out and hurried down the stairs, Holmes sat up, listening intently. He heard the front door slam shut and scrambled to his feet.

"All right, Watson!" he called out.

Watson came in from the bedroom. "It worked, Holmes!"

"So far, so good," Holmes said.

"You think that Moran will come himself to...to...?"

"To administer the *coup de grâce*?" Holmes nodded. "He's not going to miss a chance like this. He'll be over in next to no time. So, Watson—"

"Yes...yes?"

"Back to your post with gun at the ready," Holmes instructed, urging Watson back to the bedroom. "Moran believes me to be alone and at death's door."

Bending down he sprawled on the floor as before, tensing as he heard the front door opening and slamming.

"Stand by, Watson!" he whispered loudly. As the footsteps sounded outside the door he began groaning and coughing.

"Help...help, someone."

Colonel Moran entered the room cautiously, but with a purposeful tread.. He was a big man, wearing an expensive suit. Hatless, he carried his 'gun-stick' over his left arm.

Crossing quickly to Holmes, he stood staring down at him with a triumphant expression.

"So...Sherlock Holmes, we meet again!"

"Help me," Holmes groaned from where he still lay on the floor, apparently not seeing Moran.

Moran grinned crookedly. "Oh, I'll help you...." He prodded Holmes with his foot. "It's Moran...here to send you to join Moriarty!"

Holmes raised himself slightly, as if realizing for the first time who was addressing him. "Moran! *You!*"

Moran aimed his gun-stick at Holmes, then changed his

mind, looking about him. "But, no...I won't waste another bullet on you."

He reached out a hand and took a cushion from off the nearest chair.

"This will put a stop to your groaning!" he said viciously, and bent down, intent on suffocating Holmes with the cushion.

Instantly Holmes reached up and dragged him down, at the same time getting to his feet, and reversing the situation.

He held Moran tightly in a jujitsu grip, and called out urgently: "Watson!"

Watson came rushing in from the bedroom, revolver levelled at Moran. "All right, Moran!" he snapped.

"Get up," Holmes told Moran, releasing him from his grip. "We won't shoot you down, like a dog."

He pulled off the mask and threw it on the table.

"Put your hands up and keep them up!" Watson waved the revolver at Moran. He got slowly to his feet and raised his hands.

Holmes stooped and picked up the gun-stick, and hooked it over his own arm.

Moran instinctively lowered his hands, attempting to reach for his gun. "That's mine!" he snarled.

"Keep your hands up!" Watson warned sharply. "Or I'll...."

Moran spun to face Watson, arms wide apart, as if daring him to shoot.

"Dr. Watson...surely not? When your sole purpose for existence on this troubled planet is to save life...not destroy it."

Watson's expression betrayed that the words had clearly disturbed him, and he turned to Holmes for guidance.

The detective did not answer, his attention remaining fixed on Moran, who now turned to him and spoke softly:

"While, at the same time, I'm sure, you can explain to your bloodthirsty friend, what will surely happen, should he carry out his homicidal threat?"

Holmes tightened his lips with sick realization. "You have left explicit instructions that the innocent person you hold captive will be summarily dealt with."

"Philip Green!" Watson gasped. He lowered the revolver and turned to Holmes.

"So the message has got through." Moran laughed grimly. "You have lost the day, Holmes."

"Not the day; only this round."

Moran visibly relaxed. "You know, your lack of comprehension of the facts almost amuses me...you will never win.... I shall avenge Moriarty...you killed him." He began backing to the door. "So be warned, Holmes.... And...," he pointed to the gun-stick, "I'll have *that* back, I swear it."

After the door slammed, Watson rushed towards it, and shouted after Moran. "You murderous swine!"

Moments later the front door downstairs slammed shut.

"Save your breath, Watson," Holmes told him. The doctor turned back to his friend dejectedly.

Holmes took back his revolver, and returned it to the writing desk.

"What can we do?" Watson asked, as Holmes calmly produced his pipe, refilling it, and lighting up.

Watson slumped dejectedly into a chair, his eyes on Holmes.

"First," Holmes mused, "let us count our blessings, so to speak. See what I have achieved in my client's interests, since taking on the case this morning." He looked at Watson sharply. "Only this morning, d'you realize that?"

"Of course, you've done splendidly." Watson's dejection belied his words.

Holmes smiled faintly. "Ah, I beg your pardon, I should have phrased that more generously...it is what *we* have achieved, my dear Watson."

Watson perked slightly. "Oh, I did nothing.... I simply followed your instructions."

Holmes clapped him on the shoulder. "No, you acted with determination and the highest courage."

"Oh, my dear chap, really!"

"We have rescued Lady Frances from the clutches of the Shlessingers," Holmes went on incisively, "and, at the same time, totally destroyed Milverton's vile scheme to blackmail her...." He broke off at the sound of the front door opening downstairs.

The voice of Mrs. Hudson called up to them. "I'm back, Mr. Holmes."

Holmes crossed to the door, and called down to his house-keeper. "Thank you, Mrs. Hudson."

"I left the lady safe and well," she called up to him.

"Splendid," Holmes said approvingly. "And now, could you do something else, please?"

"I know what you're going to say," Mrs. Hudson chuckled. "Bring you and Dr. Watson a fresh pot of tea."

"You are worthy of stardom as a mind reader on the music halls, Mrs. Hudson," Holmes called down.

"Oh, Mr. Holmes!" Mrs. Hudson bustled off to her kitchen

"Tea, Holmes!" Watson expostulated. "But surely we should be planning our next move!"

"We are," Holmes spoke calmly. "We're regrouping our resources to mount another...and successful...attack."

Watson let out a sigh, relaxing. "Oh...yes, well, perhaps a cup of tea is a good idea."

Holmes relit his pipe, which had gone out. "One hazard we hadn't foreseen was Philip Green's involvement."

Watson gave a start. "Heavens, yes...if anything should happen to him—"

"But, even in his case, we may feel encouraged."

"Yes, we know where they've got him," Watson said, "Unless they decide to move him."

Holmes shook his head. "We've given Moran no reason to suspect what we know, and shifting Green to yet another hiding place today would present difficulties."

The voice of Mrs. Hudson sounded cheerily: "Tea on its way, Mr. Holmes!"

"Splendid!" Holmes went across to the table and cleared away the mask into the writing table drawer.

Mrs. Hudson entered with a tray with tea-things, and quickly placed the items on the table, Watson assisting.

"There we are, then," Mrs. Hudson said. "Just what the Doctor ordered! Eh, Dr. Watson?" she added archly, putting a plate of biscuits on the table. "And some of those biscuits I know you specially like."

"Thank you, Mrs. Hudson," Watson smiled.

After checking everything was in order. Mrs. Hudson turned and went out with the empty tray.

"Thank you, Mrs. Hudson," Holmes called after her, knocking his pipe out into an ashtray and returning it to his pocket.

For a moment they drank their tea appreciatively, Watson nibbling a biscuit, Holmes pacing up and down as he drank his tea, his brow wrinkled in concentrated thought. Suddenly he stopped his pacing. "That's it!"

"What is?" Watson looked up.

"My reference to Mrs. Hudson performing on the music halls...her cousin, stage door keeper at the Holborn Empire, was brutally robbed by a thug named Benskin. I got him five years."

Watson looked his puzzlement. "A criminal named Benskin who robbed Mrs. Hudson's cousin? My dear Holmes, what on earth has that to do with our problem?"

"He'd been employed as a temporary barman at the public house nearby called The Limping Man," Holmes explained. "Coincidentally, he was crippled in his right leg...and left behind a bloodstained footprint, which I was able to prove was his."

Watson was still puzzled. "I still don't see its relevance to Colonel Moran and...."

"He shouted from the dock that he'd 'get me' for putting him away." Holmes spun and pointed to the writing desk. "Watson... in the second drawer down you'll find my theatrical makeup."

Watson stared at Holmes as if he'd taken leave of his senses. "Theatrical makeup?"

Holmes crossed quickly to the wall-phone and dialled a number. Watson stood dithering, still not knowing what to make of Holmes' instructions. His puzzlement increased when Holmes added, over his shoulder: "And also a hand mirror."

"A hand mirror!" Watson muttered to himself.

Holmes spoke into the telephone: "Billy? Holmes here. A cab straight away. To the corner of Tamworth Road."

Watson turned in surprise. "Tamworth Road?"

Holmes hurried past him, into the bedroom. "Benskin was of much the same height and build as myself and, with the aid of makeup, I aim to impersonate him."

Watson was now completely nonplussed. "Impersonate— you mean...?"

"I'll need spirit-gum and some crepe hair," Holmes told him, calling from the bedroom..

"You mean, you're going to the Shlessingers, disguised as...?"

Holmes called through again from the bedroom. "In the book-shelf you'll see my rogues' gallery file...you'll find Benskin's photo."

Watson went into action promptly, and soon found sticks of makeup, and spirit-gum from a drawer, along with a false moustaches and crepe hair, which he brought to the table, pushing aside the tea-things. He found a hand mirror, which he placed on the table, and then the file in the bookcase. Opening it, he began checking the photos.

Holmes continued talking from the bedroom. "I've got some apparel appropriate for the rôle...the sort Benskin will be wearing...he'll be just out of prison...."

A moment later Holmes appeared dramatically at the bedroom door. "What d'you think, Watson?"

He was wearing a shabby suit with a cap stuffed in a pocket; a skullcap drawn over his head gave it the appearance of being close-shaven. Oddest of all was the fact that his right leg appeared shorter than the other.

Watson stared at him in utter disbelief and dropped the photo-file.

"Good God! Is it you, Holmes?"

Holmes advanced into room, limping slightly, his face contorted in an evil grimace. Several of his teeth appeared to be missing, and when he answered Watson he did so in a Cockney accent.

"Yus, I've heard it over the grapevine, Colonel Moran, as you're out to get Sherlock Bloody Holmes...'im wot got me sent down for five for a crime I never done.... I'm your man, Colonel, to help you fix the bastard good and proper!"

Watson straightened from picking up the dropped file. "It's absolutely marvellous, Holmes!"

"Now, I just need to add some touches," Holmes went on urgently, seating himself at the table.

He instructed Watson to put the photo-file on table, and searched through it find the photo he wanted, At length he gave a grunt of satisfaction.

"Here he is...Arthur Benskin full face and profile...." He placed the photo so he can copy from it, and deftly started to apply make-up, while Watson held the mirror for him.

"A touch of prison-pallor, I think will be suitable." Holmes murmured. "And, now that drooping moustache...they'd let him keep that, since it's in his mug-shots, as they're described in prison slang."

After his initial enthusiasm for Holmes' disguise, Watson began to have doubts.

"But...but you'll be putting your head in the lion's mouth."

"Not *my* head," Holmes said dryly. "Benskin's! Spirit-gum, please."

Watson handed him a brush with gum on it, which Holmes applied to his upper lip. "That moustache will do the trick, I think," Holmes muttered. He took a false moustache from Watson and applies it to his upper lip, dabbing it on carefully with a large handkerchief.

The front door rang downstairs. Holmes turned and shouted downstairs:

"That'll be Billy, Mrs. Hudson. Tell him I'm in a hurry."

"Yes, Mr. Holmes...I'll tell him," Mrs. Hudson called back.

"Mr. Holmes won't be a minute, Billy," she informed the caller after opening the door to him, "And he'll be in a hurry." She thought to herself: "Though, I must say I've never known him when he wasn't."

Upstairs Holmes moved to his writing desk and from a drawer extracted a hypodermic needle and phial.

"Holmes!" Watson cried, horrified. "No!"

Ignoring Watson's imprecations, Holmes rolled up his sleeve, expertly filled the hypodermic from a phial, and injected his forearm.

"You swore you would give it up!" Watson said accusingly.

Holmes rolled down his sleeve and returned the hypodermic and phial to the drawer. Closing it, he turned to his agitated friend.

"Do not concern yourself, Watson, I'm no Dr. Jekyll about to turn himself into a Mr. Hyde! I'm merely stimulating my histrionic powers, to give the rôle I'm about to play it fullest effect." With that he strode out of the room.

"God bless you, Holmes," Watson muttered, shaking his head.

At the foot of the stairs Holmes encountered Mrs. Hudson.

"I shan't be long, Mrs. Hudson," he told her.

"Oh, Mr. Holmes! I hardly recognized you!"

Their voices carried faintly upstairs to Watson. As he heard the front door close, he turned back to the table; then suddenly remembering something, he went across to the desk drawer.

Pulling out Holmes's revolver, he dashed to the top of the stairs and shouted down:

"Holmes! Your revolver! You've forgotten it. You've forgotten your revolver!"

CHAPTER THREE

A storm was breaking over London. Intermittent flashes of lightning were followed by rumbles of thunder. In his laboratory at the Nursing Home, Dr. Shlessinger was busy in his laboratory, handling a phial and a hypodermic syringe.

A lightning flash made him aware of the gathering darkness, and he paused in his work to switch on the laboratory light.

The light spilled through the open laboratory door into the adjacent darkened room. There came a further rumble of thunder and a distant lightning flash.

Shlessinger fingered his collar. "Phew...it's damned warm," he muttered.

Coming out of the laboratory, he crossed to the French windows, and opened one of them to let in some fresh air.

The front door bell was ringing, but a further rumble of thunder prevented Shlessinger from hearing it as he returned to his laboratory, and continued his dealings with the phial and syringe.

As the front door bell continued to ring again, more insistently, he abruptly became aware of it.

As he turned quickly to come out of the laboratory, he dropped the phial.

"Damn and blast!" he muttered, stooping to retrieve the phial.

As the front door bell continued to ring loud and long he shouted out: "All right...I hear you!"

Quickly picking up phial, he replaced it with the syringe on a laboratory bench, and hurried out of the facility, as the bell continued ringing.

Hurrying into the hall, he shouted again: "I heard you, I tell you!"

Yanking open the front door, he found Milverton glaring at him.

"What the devil's happening?" Milverton demanded impatiently. "I've been ringing for hours!"

"All right...all right," Shlessinger grumbled. "I was in the lab and I couldn't hear you for the thunder." As they crossed the hall, he switched on the lights.

Milverton looked about him. "Where's the Colonel?"

"He's not back yet...why, anything he needs to know?"

Milverton nodded. "He'll want to hear about my meeting with Holmes."

"So—how did it go?"

Before Milverton could answer, there sounded a muffled cry from the direction of the hall.

"Help...help me, *help me*, someone...." It was Philip Green, crying for help.

Milverton gave a start. "Who the devil's that?"

Shlessinger looked towards the door and shrugged. "It's Philip Green...I'm just going to give him another jab."

The French window suddenly slammed together with a bang; causing both men to jump. Quickly Shlessinger crossed the room and closed them, turning the key in the lock. "The thunder made it a bit warm in here," he explained.

Green's voice sounded again. "Help...help me...*oh, help*...."

Milverton looked down at the syringe Shlessinger was now holding. "That the same stuff you used on Lady Frances?"

"No, it's something I'm experimenting with," Shlessinger said, going to the doorway into the hall.

Milverton gave a little shudder. "Gives me the creeps, that does...."

Shlessinger looked at him cynically. "Bit squeamish, aren't we?"

"Perhaps, but...."

Shlessinger snorted. "Coming from you...a murderer of souls...as Justice Wade described one of your lot the other day, giving him ten years...!"

Milverton shrugged and remained standing at door, watching as Shlessinger crossed to one of several doors that led off from the hall and opened it.

Green screamed at him. "Help...!" he broke off, as he saw the syringe. "No...no...leave me alone...leave me alone!"

Deliberately, Shlessinger closed the door.

As he saw the closing door, the watching Milverton turned away from the doorway, and went back into the room. He took a cigarette from his case, and nervously operated his lighter.

"Perhaps I am getting squeamish," he muttered to himself. "Murderer of the soul! What nonsense...."

He stood staring into the laboratory as he drew on the cigarette, then turned expectantly as a door slammed.

Shlessinger came back into the room from the hall, still carrying the syringe.

"That's taken care of him...for the time being!"

Shlessinger turned into his laboratory and laid the syringe on a bench. Switching off the laboratory light, he rejoined Milverton, closing the door behind him.

"Pretty strong stuff, eh?" Milverton commented, aware that Green had ceased his moaning.

Shlessinger nodded. "You have to be careful not to overdo it."

"If you did," Milverton asked curiously, "would it leave any signs?"

"It wouldn't show in the blood...but you'd have to explain the needle marks!"

Milverton glanced towards the hall door. "How long can you keep him...quiet?"

Shlessinger shrugged. "As long as the Colonel requires...by the way, how *did* it go with Sherlock Holmes?"

"Oh, I'm to collect tomorrow...in return for Green's letter... so-called."

"The £10,000?"

"No cash, no deal." Milverton's tone changed. "That's what you expected me to say, isn't it?"

"Well...isn't that what he wanted to talk to you about?" Shlessinger asked.

"And you think I fell for it?" Milverton snapped.

Shlessinger looked surprised by his tone. "What...what you getting at?"

"It was just a trap," Milverton told him briefly.

"A trap...what do you mean?"

Milverton tightened his lips. "Put yourself in Holmes's shoes. He has a good idea that the letter is a fake, neither does he believe Green took off with the bonds."

"What are you telling me?" Shlessinger asked deliberately.

A flicker of lightning, and a distant rumble of thunder caused Milverton to glance at the French windows, as Shlessinger frowned to assimilate what he'd been told.

"It was a trap, set to lure the Colonel, of course," Milverton said briefly.

Shlessinger nodded slowly. "You mean, Holmes knows he's got to get Moran before Moran gets him?"

"That's it. And he's guessed the Colonel's using Philip Green as bait to trap him. At the same time, he's got to rescue Green to earn his fee from this Lady Frances."

"So that's why Moran transferred Green here?"

Milverton nodded. "And why Holmes had me followed from Baker Street."

Shlessinger gave a start. "What?

"The Cab I took just 'happened to be passing'...which was a trifle too convenient, I thought," Milverton said.

"So you neatly switched to another one, of course?"

Milverton smiled. "Better than that. I got out and walked...." He paused as there came the sound of the front door opening and shutting.

Cecilia's voice sounded from the hall. "Anyone home?" A moment later she came into the room. "Where's Moran?"

"Why?" her brother asked. "What's the news?"

She gave a mirthless smile. "Only that I left him with Sherlock Holmes...settling his fate, once and for all."

Shlessinger frowned. "What?

"Yes, what d'you mean?" Milverton demanded.

"I've just told you...," Cecilia explained calmly. "Sherlock Holmes is dead! Finished...done for!"

"Who killed him?" Milverton asked sharply.

"Ask Colonel Moran!"

"He did it?" Shlessinger gripped his sister's arm.

Cecilia nodded, quite unmoved. "He used his gun-stick, from the house opposite, then sent me over to check."

Shlessinger exhaled slowly. "Sherlock Holmes put out of business forever...."

"I saw him lying there with my own eyes, his face shattered," Cecilia affirmed. She gave a little shudder. "He wasn't a pretty sight, I can tell you. He begged me to help him."

Shlessinger smiled. "It's the most wonderful news...."

"I could have finished him off myself," Cecilia told him. "Only I daren't rob the Colonel of the pleasure!"

"So," Milverton mused, stubbing out his cigarette in an ashtray, "the great Sherlock Holmes is no more."

Shlessinger looked at his sister. "How's this going to affect our plans?"

Cecilia shrugged. "It can't be anything else but to the good." She turned to Milverton, "What's *your* news?"

"Putting the black on Lady Frances isn't going to work," Shlessinger cut in before Milverton could answer.

"What d'you mean?" Cecilia demanded angrily.

"Holmes was too smart for me," Milverton admitted. "As I was explaining, what he was after was to get me to reveal Green's hiding place."

"You didn't?"

"Of course not," Shlessinger said.

Milverton frowned. "So, we're left with Green on our hands?"

Shlessinger grunted. "Well, we can fix that."

"We'd better wait to see what Colonel Moran thinks," Milverton said.

"What *I* think," said Cecilia viciously, "is that we should give him the same treatment Holmes got. If he escaped, we'd be for it."

Milverton spread his hands, looking at Shlessinger. "How can he escape? He's doped all the time."

"Keeping him here's too risky, I tell you," Cecilia snapped.

Abruptly an anguished voice was heard just outside the door.

"Help me, someone! *Help me!*"

"What the hell...?" Shlessinger gasped as Green staggered in from the hall, shouting for help. He was utterly dishevelled, wearing trousers and shirt with canvas shoes and was clearly hysterical.

"Help me get out of here!"

Shlessinger and Cecilia grabbed him roughly. "Shut up, blast you!" Shlessinger snarled.

"I thought you were supposed to keep him quiet?" Cecilia said accusingly.

"I gave him a good jab."

"Let me go," Green moaned. "Let me out of here—"

His voice snapped off as Shlessinger slapped him heavily across the mouth, Immediately a trickle of blood appeared.

"Shut up...shut up!" Shlessinger hit him again.

Green sagged, almost knocked out,

"Quick," Shlessinger told Milverton as he stood gaping. "Give me a hand."

Milverton helped Shlessinger support Green, as Cecilia spun towards the laboratory.

"I'll soon fix him up," she muttered.

"What are you doing?" Shlessinger demanded.

Cecilia's voice sounded from inside the laboratory. "I'll soon show you."

"Not that stuff!" Shlessinger shouted. "It's deadly!"

Cecilia emerged from the laboratory, with a hypodermic syringe in her hand, obviously intent on drugging Green.

"*This'll* keep him quiet," she asserted viciously.

"Don't do it!" Milverton was thoroughly alarmed. "You'll kill him!"

Green resumed his moaning. "Help...help...get me away from here...."

"Shut up, damn you!" Cecilia pushed up the sleeve of Green's left arm, preparing to give him a jab.

"Don't let her!" Green screamed. "Don't let her do it!"

"Stop it, I tell you," Shlessinger warned.

There came a sudden flash of lightning, then a roll of thunder—and the lights went out, plunging the room into darkness.

"What the hell?" Shlessinger gasped.

"For God's sake...what's going on?" Milverton demanded.

"It's only the storm," Cecilia said scornfully.

The lights came up again slowly to reveal a tall figure standing in the doorway.

"Colonel Moran!" Shlessinger gasped.

Cecilia and Milverton turned to Moran, then Cecilia moved towards Moran, leaving Milverton struggling to support the semi-collapsed Green.

Moran came slowly into room and held out a hand to Cecilia. The woman hesitated, then handed over the hypodermic to Moran.

He dropped the syringe onto the floor, and stamped his boot on it.

"Get him back to his room," Moran growled at Milverton. Then he fixed Cecilia with a stare. "It seems that the female of the species is more deadly than the male!"

Breathing hard, Milverton dragged Green from the room.

Cecilia bent as if to pick up the broken syringe, only for Moran to step in and kick it aside with his right foot. She gave him a bitter look and turned away.

"We didn't hear you, Colonel," Shlessinger said uncertainly.

"I habitually close doors quietly." Moran said. He glared at Cecilia. "Did I order anything in the medical line?"

"It was only intended to quiet him," Cecilia said sullenly.

Shlessinger spoke enthusiastically, seeking to change the smouldering atmosphere. "Well, well, Colonel! So, we've got Sherlock Holmes out of our system, eh?"

"I was telling them how you dealt with him," Cecilia put in quickly.

Milverton came back into the room, wiping his brow with a handkerchief. "He's out like a light, but I locked the door."

Moran nodded, then turned to Cecilia. "I'm afraid Mr. Holmes is still with us."

Shlessinger's haw dropped. "What? He's alive?"

Cecilia was incredulous. "But I saw him...all that blood...."

"Holmes is very much alive," Moran said deliberately, looking at Shlessinger.

"You mean it was all a put-up job?"

Moran nodded. "Which explains why I don't want Green to come to any harm."

"You can use him...against Holmes?" Milverton asked shrewdly.

"I believe that opportunity will come my way," Moran assented.

Shlessinger wrinkled his brow. "In return for sending him back, you mean?"

Moran nodded. "I fancy Holmes would feel obliged to return my gun."

"But surely Green will go straight to the police?" Cecilia protested.

Moran shrugged. "We can't hold him forever."

"That's why if we killed him off...," Cecilia began, but Moran cut her off.

"There wouldn't be a corner of the earth where you could hide," he stated.

"My God, you're right," Milverton said.

"I must admit, I wouldn't care for the nine o'clock jump either!" Shlessinger said uneasily.

Cecilia turned away, disgusted at the other's timidity.

"It's the second time he's supposed to have been killed," Moran mused. "Over the Reichenbach Falls before. Then, today, in his own home. But next time it's going to be third time unlucky for you, Sherlock Holmes!"

Suddenly the front door bell began to ring stridently.

"Who the devil's that?" Shlessinger demanded, startled.

All those in the room became alert and tense, staring at the doorway and hall beyond.

Cecilia glanced at Moran. "Are you expecting anyone?"

Moran shook his head.

Shlessinger looked suspiciously at Milverton. "Sure you weren't followed?"

"I'm certain I wasn't."

The front door bell rang again.

Shlessinger looked worried. "If it's the police, and they find Green...."

"I *said* we should kill him!" Cecilia snapped.

"If it's the police," Milverton said, thinking, "and it's him they're after, they'll have a search warrant."

The front door bell rang again.

"I'll answer it," Cecilia decided. She turned to do so, but pulled up with a gasp as Sherlock Holmes—heavily disguised as Benskin—appeared suddenly in the doorway.

"You all deaf?" Holmes asked dryly, his voice disguised. "I bin ringin' all night."

"Who the devil are you?" Shlessinger demanded.

"Well, I ain't the Devil...that's for starters."

Cecilia glared at the intruder. "How'd you get in?"

Holmes limped into the room. "One question at a time, lady... first, I'm Arthur Benskin...just finished enjoying His Majesty's pleasure at the Scrubs. Second, I got in because there ain't no locked door nowhere can keep me out, if I wants to get in."

"A damned burglar!" Milverton exclaimed.

"'Breaking and entering', if you don't mind. And...." Holmes looked slyly at Moran, "...we're none of us damned till the Day o' Judgment. Ain't that right Colonel?"

Moran stared at Holmes. "You have the advantage of me. I don't know you."

"Nor do any of us," Shlessinger snapped. "Nor do we want to—so get out!"

"And make it fast," Cecilia added venomously, "or we'll call the police."

Holmes smiled complacently. "What, blow the gaff on one of your own kind?"

Shlessinger moved towards Holmes. "If you don't get out...."

Moran touched him on the shoulder. "All right, Shlessinger, relax." He eyed Holmes. "You claim acquaintance with me?"

Holmes smiled faintly. "Well, say a business acquaintance. Something we have in common."

"Or wouldn't it be more accurate to say 'someone'?" Moran asked deliberately. "A certain private detective named...."

"...Sherlock Holmes. Bull's-eye, Colonel." Holmes/Benskin finished.

"Who was directly responsible for your sojourn in Pentonville?" Moran hazarded shrewdly.

"Not the 'Ville, the Scrubs. Got a better outlook than the 'Ville...almost in the country."

"I must confess I'm not too familiar with either," Moran commented.

"Look, Colonel," Shlessinger said impatiently. "What's this got to do with us?"

"Yes," Milverton agreed. "It's all very interesting, but...."

"Perhaps our friend here will explain," Moran said.

"If he *is* 'our friend'," Cecilia said suspiciously.

"Well," Holmes said, "let's put it this way. You thought you'd settled Holmes's hash good and proper, only to find he'd turned the tables on you."

They all stared at Holmes for a long moment, then Moran said slowly:

"I'm sure you have reason to rely on your source of information?"

Holmes smiled. "None better than my own eyes and ears,

Colonel. Next door to 221B Baker Street is number 223—which lets accommodation at reasonable rates—and where yours truly has had a room since I came out. And my landlady, Ma Griffen, and his Mrs. Hudson, well...they has a gossip, now and then. And I listens, and I keeps my peepers peeled about the comings and goings between this house and...well...."

"Do go on," Shlessinger invited, his eyes narrowed with interest. "Surely, there's more to come?"

"Well, yes...I gets the word—over the 'grapevine', of course—which is that the Colonel and Sherlock Holmes have clashed...and I thinks, well, there might be some pickings in this for yours truly, and calls on His Nibs...."

"On Sherlock Holmes himself," Milverton said wonderingly.

"When was this?" Cecilia asked sharply.

"Soon after you'd left...." Holmes looked at Moran, waiting for him to make some reply, then resumed as Moran remained silent, "Without that special stick of yours, wasn't it, Colonel?"

The others stared at Moran, who tensed, then turned away, taking a few paces before turning back to face Holmes, his face bitter.

"*He* sent you," he rasped.

Holmes nodded calmly. "You can 'ave it back...in return for your prisoner."

Again there was a distant flash of lightning, and rumble of thunder fading into distance as Shlessinger glanced out of the French windows.

"The storm's receding," he commented.

Abruptly the distressed cries from Green resumed. Moran eyed Holmes for a long moment, then turned in the direction of Green's cries.

"Let me out...help me, some one...*help me*...!"

"Fetch him," Moran instructed Milverton.

Milverton nodded hastily, and went out.

Shlessinger looked at Moran. "It's all a bit of a coincidence, isn't it? Him meeting Holmes the way he says?"

"It's cooked up by Holmes and him.... Or he's made it all up himself," Cecilia said sourly.

"That's right...chat among yourselves," Holmes murmured amiably.

Moran made no reply and turned away. Holmes' glance followed him. Moran stayed silent as Green was heard in the hall.

"You can't keep me a prisoner...you *can't*, I tell you."

Green, followed by Milverton, entered from the hall. Milverton was holding him by his left arm. The hapless prisoner appeared shaken and broken, blood trickling from his mouth.

Moran gave Milverton his pocket handkerchief. "Clean him up."

Milverton dabbed Green's face with the handkerchief, as he continued to mutter. "Let me go...let me go free...."

"Keep quiet, and listen!" Moran growled at him. He turned to Holmes. "You're confident Holmes will make the exchange?"

Holmes shrugged. "You know him better than I do...."

Moran scowled thoughtfully. "He's always been a man of his word, that's true."

"But you're going to trust *his* word!" Cecilia burst out angrily, pointing at Holmes. "A damned jailbird!"

"Mind you don't end up one yourself." Holmes gave her a sardonic smile.

Moran ignored Cecilia's outburst, and looked at Holmes. "What's *your* reward for all this?"

"Yes, you're not doing this for nothing, I'll bet," Shlessinger said.

Holmes regarded Moran levelly. "I'm sure you can be reasonably generous, Colonel, when you want."

"What's Holmes paying you?" Shlessinger demanded impatiently.

Holmes smiled faintly. "Not as much as I expect."

Milverton frowned at Moran. "Forgive me for interrupting... but what's to prevent our friend here going straight to the police?"

"That's right," Cecilia agreed. "He can have us put away for years!"

Green had been struggling to follow the conversations, the import of which he was now just beginning to understand. "Of course I won't," he implored Moran. "All I want is to get away from here...I promise you."

Moran looked at him. "I've no alternative but to trust you."

"I swear I'll keep my word!" Green said desperately.

"You had better do that, if you want to keep your life." Moran said harshly.

"Holmes will see he doesn't open his mouth," 'Benskin' put in. "You said yourself he's a man of his word...."

"So long as his...er...client is happy," Shlessinger said.

Moran appeared to make up his mind. "You'll pick up a cab soon enough," he told Holmes. He glanced at his watch. "And be at Baker Street in half-an-hour...then back here within the hour."

Holmes nodded assent. "With a present for you from His Nibs, which reminds me...what's my present to be, Colonel?"

"£100. In two fifty-pound notes."

"Make it £150, in three fifties...and one in advance."

Moran eyed Holmes for a moment, then reached for his note case. Taking out a £50 note, he handed it to Holmes without speaking.

Holmes took the note eagerly, spat on it, and pocketed it quickly. He turned to Green.

"What are we waiting for, then? Come on." Grabbing Green by the arm, and urged him out of the room. Pausing in the doorway, he glanced back at Moran. "See you in an hour...with the goods." Pushing Green ahead of him, he went out and into the hall.

Moran stared after 'Benskin' and Green, his expression enigmatic. Cecilia crossed to doorway and stood watching them out of the front door.

As the front door slammed behind the two men, Milverton looked at Moran uneasily. "Well, is that it, Colonel?"

"It doesn't mean the cessation of hostilities between me and

Holmes, if that's what you're thinking," Moran replied harshly.

Shlessinger and his sister both looked at Moran sharply.

Milverton looked uncomfortable. "No, no. It's just that I don't see that there's any part in it for me...."

Moran looked at him with faint contempt. "You'll be finding other fish to fry, eh?"

Milverton nodded eagerly. "That's right. So, I'll be running along, then. He crossed to the door. "*Au revoir*, everyone."

He hurried out.

Moran turned to Cecilia. "Give him a few minutes; then, just in case he takes a wrong turning and ends up at Scotland Yard, follow him."

"You can count on me," Cecilia said, nodding.

Moran looked towards the door and smiled twistedly. Abruptly he called out: "And as for you, Benskin, you can take a bow for a performance to match any actor on the London stage!"

Shlessinger and Cecilia stared at him in amazement.

"What d'you mean?" Shlessinger asked

"Just that he was no more Benskin, the burglar, than I am Jack the Ripper...that was Sherlock Holmes himself!"

The Shlessingers looked at Moran open-mouthed, dumb-founded.

CHAPTER FOUR

It was early evening on the same day as Sherlock Holmes had engineered his audacious rescue of Philip Green from the Nursing Home.

In his rooms at 221B Baker Street, Colonel Moran's gun-stick lay placed prominently on Holmes' writing desk. In the room also were Dr. Watson and Lady Frances Carfax, both of whom were looking towards the adjoining bedroom door, which stood open.

Lady Frances looked very beautiful and excited as Holmes entered from the bedroom and crossed to join them.

"My razor all right, Mr. Green?" Holmes called back into the bedroom.

"Excellent. You've been most kind, a thousand thanks."

"We must have you looking your best for Lady Frances's sake," Holmes smiled, looking at Green's fiancée.

"I'm sure she's most impatient to see you," Watson added, his eyes twinkling.

"No more impatient than I am to see her." Lady Frances' eyes gleamed as she heard Green's voice from the bedroom. "And thanks, too, for lending me your raincoat." Green came into the room, buttoning the raincoat up. He stopped in pleased amazement as he saw the girl coming forward to meet him.

"So impatient, my dear Philip, that I'm here to meet you!"

Holmes and Watson stepped aside, as Lady Frances and Green embraced each other.

"Frances! Oh, this is wonderful of you!" Watson looked on,

immensely pleased, whilst Holmes gave the scene a nod of approval.

Lady Frances gently broke free of his embrace. "You must thank Mr. Holmes and Dr. Watson for conspiring with me, so we could meet like this."

"It was simply wonderful of you," Green told Holmes sincerely. "And you, too, Doctor."

"I'm glad it's been such a happy outcome for you," Holmes commented.

"And we wish you all happiness," Watson smiled. He glanced in surprise towards the window as from the street below sounded a barrel organ, playing a popular romantic song.

Green laughed. "Listen, Frances. All Baker Street knows we're happy."

"Very romantic!" Watson commented dryly, glancing at Holmes.

Lady Frances, with her arm in Green's turned to listen to the barrel organ.

"Wonderful!" she smiled.

"Absolutely marvellous!" Green looked at the faintly smiling Holmes. "I wouldn't mind betting you arranged it!"

Still smiling enigmatically Holmes joined Watson in following Lady Frances and Green out of room.

Holmes called down to Mrs. Hudson.

"Lady Frances and Mr. Green are leaving, Mrs. Hudson."

"Yes, Mr. Holmes."

As Watson and Holmes returned to the room they heard Lady Frances and Green taking their leave of Mrs. Hudson. "Thank you for all your help," Lady Frances told the house-keeper, kissing her lightly on the cheek.

"You looks lovely, Lady Frances," Mrs. Hudson told her, as she opened the front door.

As the front door closed, the barrel organ stopped playing. Inside the room Watson glanced at the window, and turned to Holmes.

"The music's stopped." Watson narrowed his eyes. "I do

believe you did arrange it." Holmes shrugged slightly and smiled. "Oh, Holmes...that was a charming thought...." He broke off, suddenly becoming serious. "Or—was it something to do with—with Colonel Moran?"

"Police agents need to be versatile, artistic, poetical, musical...," Holmes murmured,

"And that was one of them keeping an eye on things?"

Holmes shrugged again. "We're up against a very resourceful criminal."

"Then you actually expect a visit from Moran, in an attempt to get this thing back?" Watson moved to pick up the stick-gun.

"It's still loaded," Holmes warned him. Watson hastily put down the gun-stick.

"And when will he show his hand? This evening?"

"For him," Holmes answered gravely, "any other time except this evening will be too late."

"But, of course, you'll refuse to hand it over?"

Holmes shook his head. "I doubt very much I'll be given the opportunity to refuse or otherwise."

"My dear fellow!" Watson was thoroughly alarmed. "What are you doing to defend yourself? I mean, you're in danger!"

Holmes nodded towards the window. "I've already had a word with Lestrade."

"Lestrade? You've called in Scotland Yard?"

"Certainly I have," Holmes explained. "After all, it's a kind of criminal conspiracy involving Milverton and the Shlessingers."

"Yes. Oh, that dreadful so-called nurse...."

"As well as the Colonel," Holmes added. "It's—" he broke off as the front door bell rang downstairs. "That should be Lestrade." He crossed to the door, opened it, and called down to Mrs. Hudson. "That'll be Detective Inspector Lestrade, Mrs. Hudson."

"Don't sound like him, Mr. Holmes," her voice came back. "He allus rings three times when he's expected...short, sharp ones."

"That's so." Holmes thought for a moment, then called down:

"Anyhow, answer the door and tell me who it is."

"Yes, Mr. Holmes." Mrs. Hudson opened the front door, then frowned as she saw who the visitor was. "Oh, it's *you* again."

"Good evening, Mrs. Hudson. Mr. Charles Augustus Milverton, at your service."

Mrs. Hudson was unimpressed by the man's unctuous tone. "Oh, yes?"

"Mr. Holmes is not expecting me, but—"

Watson had joined Holmes at the top of the stairs, where the voices downstairs reached clearly. He exchanged a look with Holmes. "It's Milverton! What can *he* want?"

Holmes called down: "He can come up, Mrs. Hudson, then to Watson he added: "Wait in the bedroom, if you would. He probably thinks I'm alone, anyway."

"Good idea," Watson assented, and vanished into the bedroom.

"You can go on up," Mrs. Hudson said shortly.

"Thank you, dear madam," Milverton murmured, and started to climb the stairs to Holmes' room on the landing.

Milverton entered through the open doorway, and found Holmes standing by his writing desk. On it lay the gun-stick, its butt end pointing towards the door.

"Mr. Holmes, good evening. It's most kind of you to permit me to call."

"What d'you want?" Holmes said briefly.

Milverton indicated the gun-stick. "My visit is to do with that thing's owner, as it happens."

"If you mean Colonel Moran, he no longer owns it."

"Nevertheless, he is anxious to have possession of it once more."

"Has he deputed you to make an offer?" Holmes asked sharply.

Milverton shook his, head. "Let me explain. This afternoon, the Colonel received a visit from a criminal named Benskin, who claimed you'd hired him to do a deal on the basis that you'd exchange the gun-stick for Philip Green's release. Am I right?"

"I hear what you say," Holmes replied guardedly.

"Then hear this!" Milverton's smooth voice took on a tone of sharp urgency. "Despite any deal you may or may not have made with him, Colonel Moran intends to double-cross you... and wipe you off the face of the earth!"

"And when does he plan this interesting event?"

"Tonight!"

"How?" Holmes asked calmly.

"I don't know," Milverton admitted. "But my guess is Shlessinger and that sister of his will be involved."

"And in return for your warning, how do you expect me to reciprocate?" Holmes asked pointedly.

"Leave me out of it!" Milverton snapped. "My attempt to blackmail Lady Frances; my association with the Shlessingers and Moran; forget it all."

Holmes smiled grimly. "You sound as if you have become somewhat scared of them."

Milverton shrugged. "I...I...well, perhaps I am becoming a little squeamish," he admitted. "Anyhow, I intend to take a holiday as far away from the aforementioned as possible."

"Very wise, Mr. Milverton." Holmes nodded. "Well...thank you for your warning. I will reciprocate by forgetting this meeting ever took place and retaining not the slightest knowledge of your whereabouts or even existence."

"Thank you," Milverton said, his voice relieved. He extended his hand, but Holmes ignored it.

"Goodbye, Milverton...and good luck." As Milverton turned to go out, Holmes added softly, almost to himself. "I think you're going to need it."

Milverton stopped and stared at Holmes for a long moment, then turned quickly and went out, leaving the door open behind him.

Holmes stepped forward and called down to Mrs. Hudson: "Mr. Milverton is leaving, Mrs. Hudson."

Mrs. Hudson looked at Milverton's hurrying figure in surprise. Without waiting for her to open the door he brushed past her and jerked it open himself.

The door slammed behind him.

On hearing it, Watson came in from the bedroom. "What an extraordinary person," he commented. "I almost began to like him!"

Holmes smiled faintly. "Your faith in human nature has always appealed to me as somewhat touching."

Watson coughed. "Well, I am a doctor...and faith is as helpful to a doctor as his stethoscope."

"Quite so," Holmes murmured.

"But what did you make of his story?"

Holmes shrugged. "It was a sincere attempt to warn me, no doubt—but, of course, I already knew Moran would make another attempt to eliminate me...as well as retrieve his stick."

"You already knew?" Watson looked his surprise.

Holmes nodded calmly. "That was precisely why I allowed him to penetrate my disguise as Benskin."

"Allowed him to penetrate your disguise?" Watson was incredulous. "You mean, after all the trouble you took?"

"Indeed, it was a triumph...he was completely duped."

Watson furrowed his brow. "You mean that all the time, you wanted him to know it was you?"

"Not all the time," Holmes admitted. "But just before my exit, I let the mask fall."

"How did you do that?"

Holmes reached into a pocket and pulled forth the £50 from his pocket. "By accepting this from him."

Watson stared. "He offered you money?"

Holmes nodded. "After a little haggling, he agreed to pay me £150...£50 on account...." He waved the £50 note, "...if I obtained his gun-stick."

Watson frowned. "I still don't follow."

"Allow me to demonstrate." With his right hand Holmes extended the £50 note. "Take this, if you would."

Watson accepted the note. "Well, it's a unique sensation...to hold such a large amount in one's hand...."

"Only temporarily, Watson!" Holmes smiled. "Now, would you, as if you were Moran, give it me." Wonderingly, Watson handed back the £50. "Now, as I take it, do you observe anything about my hand?"

Watson looked down at Holmes' hand under his nose.

"Anything special? About my fingers? As a medical man you are used to dealing with all sorts of individuals."

"Of course," Watson said. "Labourers, gentlefolk of both sexes, bank managers, greengrocers...."

"And a labourer's hand, for example...his fingernails wouldn't be as scrupulously clean as a bank-manager's?"

"His fingernails? No, of course not, they would be grubby, ill-kept."

"And a burglar's?" Holmes prompted.

"Well, they would be...." Watson broke off, staring at Holmes' right hand.

"Would you say they'd look like mine?" Holmes asked, putting on the voice he had used when posing as Benskin. "Not long out of the 'Scrubs, Guv'nor...where I was sewing mailbags all the bleedin' day."

"No, your nails are well-manicured...." Watson paused. "You deliberately showed Moran your hand, so he would realize...?"

"Precisely."

"My God, of course," Watson said. "He'll be out for revenge!"

"And to exact that revenge and retrieve his precious stick, he must face me—once again."

"Here?" Watson questioned.

Holmes nodded. "Where we faced each other a few hours back...and *this* time...."

Through the window drifted the sound of the barrel organ music they had heard before, only more distant.

"That barrel organ again," Watson exclaimed. "Only it's not in Baker Street. It's in the street behind us."

Holmes tensed. "Yes...."

"Pity he doesn't know another tune,"

Holmes smiled, "It is rather."

Watson glanced at Holmes sharply. "Why, it's another signal!"

The front door bell sounded again, this time with three short rings.

Mrs. Hudson called up from the hall. "That'll be the Inspector this time, Mr. Holmes."

Mrs. Hudson opened the door, admitting Lestrade. "Good evening, Inspector."

"'Ello, Mrs. H." Lestrade said briskly. As usual, he exuded purposeful self-confidence. "'Ere we are again."

"You can go on up," the housekeeper told him.

"Yes, I knows I'm expected, Mrs. H." Lestrade strode forward and began ascending the stairs. "It's Lestrade of the Yard," he called up, and began whistling the tune played on the barrel organ.

Reaching Holmes' room he entered quickly. "Good evening, Mr. Holmes—ah! And Dr. Watson, 'ere we are again, then."

"Good evening." Holmes and Watson responded in unison.

"Oh, by the way," Lestrade went on briskly, "I'm reliably informed, the Hon. Philip Green and his piece of crackling left, both wreathed in smiles and full of the joys of Spring."

"Thanks to the efforts of Mr. Holmes on their behalf," Watson remarked, as the sounds of the barrel organ outside died away.

Lestrade smiled. "Ah, well, that's the best of being a private 'tec...no superiors to get under yer feet."

"What's the news, Inspector?" Holmes asked sharply.

"My officers duly raided the Nursing Home," Lestrade told him, "only to find the Shlessingers...brother and sister...have vamoosed, cleared out, skipped the country. They left a note, saying in so many words they would be absent for a long time."

"Gone abroad?" Watson hazarded.

"Ah—that's what they want us to believe, Doc, but of course, Lestrade of the Yard has got his ear to the ground...and I don't want no jokes about take care I don't get it trodden on!" He glared at Holmes as the detective smiled faintly and shrugged. "And," he resumed, "my men are hot on the scent of the said absconding couple...." He broke off as he noticed Holmes was now glancing at the ceiling. "What's up?" he asked, puzzled.

"D'you hear something?" Holmes asked sharply.

Watson looked up. "Footsteps," he said.

Lestrade craned his neck upwards. "I didn't hear anything...."

"Definitely footsteps," Holmes told him. "In the room above."

They listened intently, then Watson broke the silence. "They've stopped. I didn't know Mrs. Hudson let any other rooms, Holmes."

"She has this evening."

Lestrade frowned. "Who to?"

"Listen!" The other two men joined Watson in gazing up again, listening intently.

"You're right," Lestrade said. "Someone's up there, no mistake. Let's get Mrs. H. up and find out who." Crossing quickly to the doorway, he called down: "Mrs. H.—would you come up?"

There was no response.

"I think if *I* asked her, it would be better," Holmes said.

"Oh, sorry, Mr. Holmes...I didn't mean to...only, I'm anxious to know!"

Holmes called down: "Mrs. Hudson!"

"Her Master's Voice!" Lestrade muttered,

"Yes, Mr. Holmes?" the housekeeper responded, after a short pause.

"Would you come up here for a moment, please?"

"Right away, Mr. Holmes."

"The footsteps have stopped now," Watson remarked, glancing up again.

"Mrs. H. should know something about those footsteps," Lestrade remarked.

"They sounded like a woman's footsteps to me," Watson said.

"Yes, Mr. Holmes?" Mrs. Hudson asked, entering the room.

"Someone's occupying the room above," Holmes told her briefly. "I didn't know you let other rooms?"

Mrs. Hudson appeared shocked. "What? Let other rooms?

Oh, my goodness...oh, dear me." She was clearly upset.

Watson crossed to her quickly. "It's all right, Mrs. Hudson."

"Oh, my goodness! I don't let other rooms...I mean...the gentleman you heard must be one of Ma Griffen's at 223."

"They sounded like a woman's footsteps," Lestrade said.

"A lady's?" Mrs. Hudson shook her head emphatically, clearly flustered. "Oh, no, she only lets to gents. You see, she... Ma Griffen...oh, dear me...."

"Don't feel upset," Holmes advised her gently. "Just take it calmly."

Watson offered Mrs. Hudson a chair, but she shook her head and remained standing.

"She's gone and let a room...at 223...to a young chap and his brother for the evening."

"What were their names?" Lestrade asked sharply.

"I don't know...she never said. They only want the room for this evening, you see...they told her they were catching the midnight to Edinburgh."

"Could be the Shlessingers," Lestrade commented.

Holmes raised an eyebrow. "You think so?"

"Why not?" Lestrade said. "The sister could have dressed as a man."

Holmes turned to Mrs. Hudson. "You didn't see them yourself, I suppose?"

"No...she told me earlier. What are they doing in my house?" Mrs. Hudson frowned. "Oh, won't I have something to say to Ma Griffen, I can tell you!"

"How did they get in upstairs?" Lestrade said impatiently. "That's the point!"

Mrs. Hudson considered for a moment, then said: "Well, you see, there's a way across the roof from 223, and there's always been a faulty catch to that window what's never got properly mended...but I'll see to it, I promise, Mr. Holmes...oh, my goodness...to think of strangers upstairs—"

Holmes clapped a hand on her shoulder. "Don't worry about it. Just carry on as if nothing has happened."

"Yes," Watson encouraged. "Make yourself a nice cup of tea."

Lestrade puffed himself a little. "That's right, Mrs. H. Just leave everything to Lestrade of the Yard."

Mrs. Hudson looked at him. "Well! I do feel a bit of an 'eadache, coming on...."

Watson urged her gently towards the door. "I can give you some aspirin."

"No, no, Dr. Watson...thanks ever so. Just a cup of tea, and I'll be all right." As she descended the stairs, she continued muttering to herself: "Oh, dear...oh, fancy them getting into my house like that...."

Lestrade looked confidently at Holmes. "Well, for my money, Ma Griffen's 'young man' is the Shlessinger female, while big brother waits for her at 223. Her dirty deed accomplished, they heads for destination unknown."

Holmes shrugged. "If you think so."

Watson looked questioningly at Holmes, who shook his head.

Lestrade turned to the door. "So, I just nips along and picks up Shlessinger, and see him off in my Sergeant's loving care—and back pronto to help you deal with Miss Male Impersonator." He jerked his thumb at the ceiling.

Just then the telephone rang.

Lestrade stopped and turned to Holmes. "It may be my Sergeant...."

At Holmes' nod, Lestrade answered the telephone. "Lestrade of the Yard here," he said, then listened to the caller for a moment. "What time was this?" he asked sharply. "Where did the incident take place?" Pause. "Well, it's as good a spot as any. Thanks, Sergeant. I'll be along in a minute." Lestrade turned to Holmes, still holding the phone. "We'll have no more trouble with Milverton."

"Why, what's happened?" Watson asked.

"Been discovered in Melcombe Street, flat on his face, expiring his last."

Watson gave a start. "Murdered, d'you mean?"

"Considering he'd been shot in the back, it's not being treated as a case of suicide," Lestrade said dryly. "Incidentally, a young man was seen running away from the place at the relevant time."

"A young man?" Watson frowned.

Lestrade raised the telephone. "You still there, Sergeant...? Pick up big brother, now. Yes, now...charge him with being an accessory to Milverton's come-uppance. Got it?" He hung up, then, as a sudden thought struck him, he gave a quick look at Holmes and continued talking as if he was still on the telephone. "Wait a second, Sergeant...a cunning thought's occurred." He darted another look at Holmes and glanced again at the ceiling. Raising his voice, he added: "I'll be round pronto myself to see big brother on his way, and put out a search for the 'young man seen running away from the murder at the relevant time.' Got it, Sergeant? Good." Still speaking loudly he continued: "Well, Mr. Holmes, I'll nip round to 223 to see big brother on his way, and pick up his sister. So you can take it easy and all rest safe in your beds tonight."

Holmes and Watson played up to Lestrade's stratagem, also speaking clearly.

"Good work, Inspector; we're most grateful to you."

"Hear, hear!" Watson added heartily.

"Been a pleasure, I'm sure." Lestrade exited noisily, calling over his shoulder at the door. "Any time you got a problem, just send for Lestrade of the Yard." He called out to Mrs. Hudson: "Bye, bye, Mrs. H. Hope your headache's better."

"Oh, it is, Inspector, ever so much."

"Sleep safe and sound, Mrs. H."

Upstairs, Watson heard the front door open and shut. He looked at Holmes, speaking normally, "The only thing that worries me now is Colonel Moran."

"What about him?"

"Well, what's he up to? I can't believe he's given up trying to get his damned stick back."

Holmes made no reply. Switching off the main light, he plunged the room into semi-darkness, and urged Watson into the bedroom, leaving the door half open. Then taking a small revolver out of his pocket, he half opened the main door to the landing, and positioned himself behind it.

Outside in Baker Street, a hooting taxi rattled past. Very slowly, the door began to open further. It stopped for a moment, then opened a bit more before stopping. As it opened wider Colonel Sebastian Moran moved silently as a shadow into the room.

Holmes flattened himself against the wall, gun in hand, his eyes fixed on Moran, who glided into the room.

At the same moment Lestrade appeared silently in the doorway behind the intruder, his attention fixed on Moran, who was now moving on tiptoe to the writing desk.

As Moran made a grab for the gun-stick, Holmes stepped quickly behind him, and rammed his gun in the man's back.

At the same moment Lestrade closed with Moran. The tussle caused the gun-stick to go off with loud report, a bullet slamming into the wall just above the bedroom door.

Lestrade, benefitting from the element of surprise and Holmes' move with the revolver, succeeded in throwing Moran's gun to the floor, and dragging his hands behind him. There followed the clink of handcuffs being applied.

Watson appeared from the bedroom. Somewhat shakily, he looked towards the grimly smiling Yard man.

"I am Inspector Lestrade of Scotland Yard and I arrest you Colonel Sebastian Moran, on a charge of conspiracy to cause the death of Charles Augustus Milverton...."

"You all right, Watson?" Holmes questioned.

Watson managed a nod. "So it wasn't Shlessinger or his sister," he said.

"Never fear, Doctor," Lestrade spoke confidently. "I'll pick them up in no time."

"I had nothing to do with it," Moran snarled. "That murderous bitch took it into her head—"

"...And an attempt on the life of Dr. John H. Watson," Lestrade finished implacably.

Watson glared at Moran as he moved in front of him, bent down and picked up the gun-stick. He handed it to Holmes as he moved across to face Moran.

Suddenly Holmes broke the gun-stick savagely over his knee and threw the ends at Moran's feet.

Moran recoiled as if he'd been struck. "I'll see you in Hell for that, Holmes. I'll see you in Hell!"

Lestrade jerked the handcuffed Moran round to face the door. "Take it easy, Colonel—take it easy. You won't be seeing anyone in Hell for a long time, though they'll give you a taste of it in Dartmoor."

As he was forced through the door, his cuffed hands behind his back, Moran turned and shouted at Holmes: "You haven't seen the last of me, damn you, Holmes! We'll meet again...and next time...!"

Watson stooped to pick up the broken gun-stick, and put the pieces into the wastepaper basket. "*What* a day it's been," he mused. "A beautiful woman being blackmailed...her fiancé kidnapped...Milverton shot by that dreadful so-called nurse... and Moran creeping about, and damn near murdering me!"

As he was speaking Holmes crossed to the writing desk, and took out the hypodermic and phial from the drawer. He hesitated for a long moment, then replaced them and closed drawer with a snap.

As Watson watched him intently, he picked up his violin, and started playing the same tune as that had been played on the barrel organ....

ABOUT THE AUTHOR
(1908-2006)

by Philip Harbottle

Born in July 1908 in Dudley, Worcestershire as Vivian Ernest Coltman-Allen, Ernest Dudley grew up in Cookham, Berkshire, where his father kept a hotel. Stanley Spencer lived next door, and was a friend of the family. Through Spencer's patrons, the hotel became a meeting place for artists and actors. Ivor Novello was a weekend fixture. The comedian and film star Jack Buchanan helped the young Ernest rehearse a song for an amateur concert.

At the age of seventeen Ernest left boarding school and joined a theatre company touring Shakespeare through provincial Ireland, in village halls and cowsheds. From this he graduated to the more upscale Charles Doran Company, and performed in proper theatres, paying its actors the munificent sum of £2 a week. For the rest of life he used and was known by his stage name of Ernest Dudley

Always one with an eye for the ladies, Ernest soon met and teamed up with his late wife, the celebrated actress Jane Grahame.

Jane came from a theatrical family: her stepfather was Ellie Norwood, famous silent film actor who played Sherlock Holmes on stage. Through these family connections, Ernest secured work in the West End, appearing with Charles Laughton and Fay Compton, amongst others. When the original production of Noel Coward's *PRIVATE LIVES* transferred to Broadway, it was he and his wife who were recruited to take over the Laurence Olivier and Gertrude Lawrence roles in the British touring production.

His wife regularly played leading roles in the stage plays of Edgar Wallace, and Ernest would later create for her the character of Miss Frayle, assistant to Dr. Morelle in his radio plays. Other actresses would later take over the role. Most notably Sylvia Sims. Amongst the actors who played the good Doctor was Cecil Parker.

In the 1930s and 1940s he worked regularly for the BBC. In July 1942 his famous detective character (modelled on the autocratic film actor Eric von Stronheim, who he had met in Paris in the 1930s) 'Dr. Morelle' made his radio debut on *MONDAY NIGHT AT EIGHT*. Dr. Morelle was a big hit with listeners, and engendered a long cycle of novels and short stories, a play and a film, and three series on radio. At around the same time, he launched another very successful radio programme, *THE ARMCHAIR DETECTIVE*, which ran for many years, and Ernest became known as "The BBC Armchair Detective." In this weekly programme he reviewed the best of the current releases of detective novels, dramatising a chapter from each. They included his dramatization of John Russell Fearn's 1947 novel *ONE REMAINED SEATED*, and it was this fact that would cause Fearn's biographer Philip Harbottle to seek Dudley out some fifty years later, to become his friend and agent. Notable amongst his many other radio credits is the fact that he was the first-ever radio jazz critic. In the 1950s he transferred to BBC television with an early audience participation programme, *Judge for Yourself.*

Back in the 1930s Ernest also ran a parallel career as a newspaper journalist, specialising and pioneering in show business gossip, working for a time with Val Guest, with whom he had also earlier worked as a film scriptwriter in the British "quota" studio system. Amongst his many newspaper 'scoops' was how he had collaborated with actor Fred Astaire in a London night-club on the creation of a new dance-step.

All of which only gives the bare bones of an amazing career as, variously, an actor, sports correspondent, jazz critic, playwright, novelist, gossip columnist, screenwriter and crime reporter. Most amazing is the fact that he became a marathon runner at an age when other people were drawing their pensions and relaxing by the fireside, and competed in several New York Marathons, writing a best selling book on how he achieved his amazing feats, *RUN FOR YOUR LIFE*.

Apart from some fourteen Dr. Morelle books, Ernest also published during his lifetime a dozen other detective novels, mostly notably *THE HARASSED HERO* (1951) which was subsequently filmed. He also appeared with short stories in leading detective periodicals such as *John Creasey Mystery Magazine* and, in the U.S.A., *Ellery Queen Mystery Magazine*. In the 1960s, and the following decades, he became established as the author of a long series of "animal" books for children, including *RANGI*, the story of a Highland rescue dog, and *RUFUS: THE STORY OF A FOX*. Ernest has also written novelisations of a number of films, along with a range of best-selling non-fiction books on diverse subjects, most notably *CHANCE AND THE FIRE HORSES* (Harvill Press, 1972) bringing to life Victorian London and telling the story of a dog, famous at the time, called Chance, who became attached to the fire brigade, and a favourite of the Prince of Wales.

An expert and enthusiast on the exploits of Sherlock Holmes because of his wife's family connections, Ernest wrote a two-act stage play, *THE RETURN OF SHERLOCK HOLMES*, which was successfully staged and taken on tour in 1993, with Michael Cashman as Holmes.

In 2002 a US publisher, Wildside Press, began to reprint some of his best detective novels, including a number of 'Dr. Morelle' adventures, in print on demand paperback format, available online. In 2005, the leading English publishers of 'large print' editions, F. A. Thorpe, began featuring Ernest's detective novels, in their Linford Mystery series, including the 'Dr. Morelle' books. All fourteen Morelle titles were quickly reprinted, followed by a number of new posthumous short story collections compiled by his friend and agent Philip Harbottle. These contained several unpublished Morelle short stories discovered in the author's effects, plus novelizations of radio and stage scripts.

Ernest continued writing right up to the end of his life. His last novelette, 'The Beetle', featuring Edgar Allan Poe's famous detective Auguste Dupin, was based on an earlier play broadcast on BBC radio, entitled *The Flies of Isis*. The new story was accepted for a Canadian anthology of Poe's 'Dupin' stories, alongside pastiche stories by John Dickson Carr and Charles Dickens. Ernest was checking the proofs in hospital at the time of his death. The anthology was fated not to appear, but 'The Beetle' has now been included in his new posthumous detective story collection, *DEPARTMENT OF SPOOKS*.

He is survived by his only daughter, Susan Dudley-Allen, a resident of New York in the U.S.A., who is devotedly overseeing the restoration of an amazing literary career.

Lightning Source UK Ltd.
Milton Keynes UK
UKHW011912170519
342876UK00001B/58/P

NEW CASES
FOR DR. MORELLE

Cynthia Mason, a young heiress, lives with her violent stepfather, Samuel Kimber, who only holds control of her fortune while she remains unmarried. On announcing her engagement to Peter Lorrimer, a local writer, who is calling to take her away that same evening, she fears his reaction.

Lorrimer arrives and goes to talk with Kimber in his study. Cynthia, meanwhile, carrying a suitcase, tiptoes downstairs, opens the front door, and leaves....

But she's not in Lorrimer's car when he goes down to the gates after his interview with Kimber. Instead, she vanishes without a trace!

Her confidante and friend Miss Frayle, secretary to the criminologist Doctor Morelle, tries to find her—and herself becomes a target for murder!

Four classic crime stories resurrected for a brand new audience.

Borgo Press Books by ERNEST DUDLEY

Department of Spooks: Stories of Suspense and Mystery
Dr. Morelle Investigates: Two Classic Crime Tales
Dr. Morelle Meets Murder: Classic Crime Stories
New Cases for Dr. Morelle: Classic Crime Stories
The Return of Sherlock Holmes: A Classic Crime Tale

NEW CASES FOR DR. MORELLE

CLASSIC CRIME STORIES

ERNEST DUDLEY

Edited by Philip Harbottle

THE BORGO PRESS

MMXII

NEW CASES FOR DR. MORELLE

FIRST BORGO PRESS EDITION

Published by Wildside Press LLC

www.wildsidebooks.com

DEDICATION

For Ray Norton

CONTENTS

THE CASE OF THE
MISSING HEIRESS

It was early morning in London. A car was quickly threading its way through the traffic, As the car swung round a corner, the single woman passenger gazed anxiously out of the window, alternating with glancing at her watch.

At length the car drew up at the kerb outside a house in Harley Street.

Miss Frayle jumped out hastily, paid the driver, and hurried up the steps. She winced slightly as she read the name on the plate by the front door:

DR. MORELLE

She opened door with her key, and hurried into the hall. She was an attractive, rather ingenuous looking blonde in her middle twenties. Clearly flustered, she whipped off her hat, and quickly gathered her hair into a bun, pinning it in position. Then she took out of her handbag a pair of thick-rimmed library spectacles, put them on and approached a door in the hallway.

As she knocked, she braced herself for an unpleasant reception.

Doctor Morelle's study was a very large room, high-ceilinged and almost completely lined with glass-fronted bookshelves filled with medical books in several languages.

The doctor's desk was a huge mahogany one. A smaller, typist's desk in the other corner served for Miss Frayle. Against

the inner wall was the usual relaxing couch of the psychiatrist.

Miss Frayle entered the familiar room timidly, almost on tiptoe. Instantly, a deep, authoritative voice assailed her:

"My dear Miss Frayle, if I were to observe that I am even remotely interested in whatever laboured form of excuse you are about to offer for your lateness, it would be an overstatement."

"I'm most terribly sorry. I...."

"I gather from the reek of glandular extract from the civet cat, coupled with the unnatural glossiness of your hair, that you consider a permanent wave more important than transcribing my casebook!"

As usual, Miss Frayle withered under his fire.

"But, doctor, I...."

"Humanity, Miss Frayle, will not agree with you. Kindly fetch your notebook and begin to take my dictation."

Doctor Morelle was lean, with a high forehead and shrewd piercing eyes. A pompous studied manner underlined the natural grace of a man who had been European Fencing Champion for three successive years. With controlled impatience, his eyes followed Miss Frayle as she went to her desk to fetch her notebook and pencil.

He selected a cigarette from a box, leaned back in his chair, and reflectively sent a puff of smoke ceilingwards as she seated herself near to his desk.

"We will call this next episode the Case of the Missing Heiress. It is chiefly remarkable for the fact that my assistant, Miss Frayle, featured prominently in it...."

Miss Frayle alerted with flattered excitement.

"...and by her entirely inept efforts hampered me considerably in arriving at the solution of the problem."

Miss Frayle relapsed into disappointment.

"...Barren Tor, as its name suggests, is situated in the West Country. It is a lonely and isolated mansion, two miles from the nearest village, three from a Railway Station, and far removed

from any bus route. To reach the house, you turn off the main Exeter Road at Gibbett Corner...so-called from the bodies of Monmouth's rebels, which used to dangle here in chains when the notorious Judge Jeffreys stayed at Barren Tor for the Assizes...."

Miss Frayle gave a little shudder as she recalled the events of the case. Her pencil began to press a little harder onto the notepaper.

"...There is a drive nearly half a mile in length leading to the north front of the house, behind which, on the evening of October 15th, at about seven o'clock, the curtain is rising on the grim drama of Cynthia Mason...."

* * * * * * *

Samuel Kimber, Cynthia's stepfather, was seated by the fire in his wheelchair. He was an unpleasant man, of schizoid tendencies, whose lack of self-control was only equalled by his dictatorial attitude to his stepdaughter.

Cynthia was seated with him in his study, an expression of anger and dismay crossing her face as she listened to him. Abruptly she got to her feet.

"I've heard enough! I'm leaving!"

Kimber gesticulated angrily as Cynthia made to leave the room.

"Cynthia!" he shouted. "Where do you think you are going? Come back—do you hear me? Come back at once!"

The distraught girl ignored him and swept out of the room.

Kimber's manservant Bensall appeared in the doorway through which Cynthia had departed.

"Come back!" Kimber yelled after her. "Do as you're told! Come back here!" He glared at Bensall.

"Follow her, Bensall. See what she's up to, the little fool."

Bensall, his face expressionless gave a slight nod, turned and closed the door.

Outside, Cynthia hurried down the drive. It was almost pitch

black, the gloom only slightly alleviated by the light coming from a couple of windows where there was a chink in the curtains. Fearfully, she glanced over her shoulder, and stopped as an owl hooted dismally.

The moon appeared from a break in the clouds and its pale light picked out her distraught face, while the shadow of branches swaying in the wind passed across it.

Tense with fear and anxiety, she stood listening intently. She could distinctly hear the sounds of someone making their way through the undergrowth.

With a muffled exclamation of fear, Cynthia turned and started running.

She ran desperately into the night, moving swiftly along familiar paths. After what seemed an eternity, but was actually only a few minutes, she came to a small, two-storey cottage.

She gave a little gasp of relief as she saw a light in the downstairs window where the curtains had not been completely drawn. Breathing hard, she stumbled up to the front door, gasping for breath.

Inside the cottage, Peter Lorrimer, a dark-haired, good-looking, but weak-faced young man was seated at his desk, writing.

At the thunderous knock on the door, he rose and crossed the room to the door.

He opened the door to admit Cynthia, who staggered in, pushed the door shut and leaned against it.

"Cynthia!" he exclaimed.

"Oh, Peter...," she panted. "Oh, Peter...I'm so...frightened.... I had to come to...you!"

"Darling! What's frightened you?"

"It's my stepfather. He's getting worse and worse."

"Has he been shouting at you again?" Peter patted her had.

"I tried to tell him...about us...wanting to get married...but he started screaming at me...one of these days he'll kill me, Peter!"

"Nonsense, darling. You're all upset!"

Cynthia shook her head. "It's true, Peter. It's the money,

Peter. He just can't face paying out my inheritance."

Peter frowned. "But he's got to...by law...now that you are twenty-one...it's in your mother's will."

"He won't do it. He'll kill me first. That's why I told him tonight...."

She broke off and turned away. Peter followed her, gripped her arms gently so that she faced him again.

"Told him what?"

"That if he'd give his consent to our getting married, he could keep the money. I wouldn't claim it. All I want is you, Peter.... I love you. I don't care how poor we are...."

Peter moved his grip and hugged her shoulders. "I couldn't let you do that, darling. I can't support you. My writing barely brings in anything yet. There must be some other way."

"There isn't any other way," Cynthia said dispiritedly. "I daren't go back to him. Take me away, Peter. To London... anywhere...then perhaps he'll leave us in peace."

"But, dear, you've got nothing with you!" Peter pointed out. "We can't go off leaving him all your possessions into the bargain!"

Cynthia handed him an envelope. "I've brought these. It's mother's will and mine, and my papers.... I didn't want him to get these...."

Peter went to his desk, and quickly looked through the papers, At length he put the papers down on the desk, and stood for a moment, lost in thought. Then he crossed back to her.

"Listen, darling, I'll tell you what we'll do. You go back to the house—"

Cynthia interrupted him. "I daren't. I'm too frightened!"

Peter ignored her words and went on: "—and tell your stepfather I'm coming to see him this evening, in an hour. While you're doing that I'll pack a bag, and get the car out and come round to the gates at the bottom of the drive. I'll leave the car there and come up to the house."

"But supposing he refuses to see you?"

"He'll see me all right." Peter was confident. "Directly I'm

with him, run upstairs, pack a bag, put all your valuables in it, and get out of the house without being seen, and down to the car."

"But if you're there, why can't I wait for you?"

"In case I fail. I'm going to take you away, darling, whatever happens. But at any rate, we'll put up a fight for your inheritance!"

Cynthia threw her arms round his neck.

"Oh, Peter, nothing else matters to me, only you!"

"And you know it's the same with me, my sweet!" He kissed her softly. "Now, hurry, darling. We haven't a moment to lose. Only an hour, and then we'll be together—always."

He took her to the door and opened it.

A shaft of light shone out from the open door as Cynthia moved off into the darkness, while Peter remained in the doorway, looking after her. Suddenly he tensed as he caught sight of an approaching figure, a sinister silhouette against the light from the doorway. Peter stepped forward

"Who's there? Who's that?"

"It's only me," came the voice of Bensall.

"Bensall!" Peter was surprised. "What are you doing here?"

"Taking my dog for a walk."

Peter looked down and frowned in puzzlement. "Dog?"

"Yes, sir. At my heels—as he always is."

"There's no dog there."

"How logical you are, sir," Bensall smiled strangely. "To me he is always there. The best friend I ever had. I always take him for a walk about this time. It's become a habit, although it's fifteen years since he died. Goodnight, sir."

As Bensall moved off into the darkness, he looked back with a quizzical half-smile. Peter stared at him for a moment, tight-lipped and suspicious. Then he shrugged and went back into the house and shut the door.

Returning to the living room. Peter crossed to the desk and picked up Cynthia's papers, and began to look through them again.

* * * * * * *

Kimber and his stepdaughter were sitting at a table laid for supper. The room in which they sat was luxuriously furnished, indicating that Kimber was evidently a man of excellent, and expensive, taste.

Cynthia, white and trembling, was cowering back in her chair, looking across at Kimber—waiting, terrified, for his reaction to the news she had just told him.

Kimber's reaction was unexpected; his face was sad, brooding—almost gentle.

"My dear, you make me very sad. That you are not happy here with me I have sensed for a long time. There is little in this house to interest a young girl...."

Cynthia blinked in amazement. She had expected his reaction to be one of violent rage.

"...but I had pictured things happening differently. I had hoped that I should be able to share in your happiness—plan with you for your future—advise you—but now you want to leave at once, in the middle of the night. Leaving me here to fend for myself...a helpless cripple...after all I've done for you, all these years...."

Bensall approached the table and placed a dish of meat in front of Kimber, who looked up at him mournfully.

"Bensall—Miss Cynthia wishes to leave us tonight."

"Yes, sir."

"You are sorry, aren't you, Bensall?"

"Yes, sir."

"We shall be two lonely old men without her, Bensall."

"Yes, sir." Bensall placed the plates on the table and moved away towards the door.

Kimber lowered his head and began carving the meat. Suddenly he looked up and shouted after his manservant:

"Bensall, you've cooked this meat too much, you fool!"

Bensall turned and looked over his shoulder without expression, then continued on his way. At this, Kimber's face distorted

with rage.

"I like my meat bloody—you know that!" Suddenly he hurled the carving knife he was holding.

The knife struck the doorpost by Bensall's side and fell at his feet. He stooped and picked it up, fondling the knife for a moment.

"I will fetch a clean knife, sir," he said imperturbably, and went out, shutting the door quietly after him.

* * * * * * *

Kimber pushed his plate aside. His gaze pinned his step-daughter, who looked at him apprehensively from the other side of the table.

"What time did you say this young man was coming?" The gentleness, the crocodile tears, had now gone from his voice. His manner was highly-strung, arrogant.

"Half past eight," Cynthia said quietly.

"And his name?" Kimber asked sharply.

"Peter Lorrimer."

"And he writes, you say?" Kimber tightened his lips. "Writes what? Novels? Nonsense about romantic young men with no money who want to marry wealthy and attractive young women?"

Cynthia seemed on the point of tears at his withering sarcasm, and seeing this, Kimber changed his tone to a more ingratiating one.

"Cynthia, when you marry, you'll be a rich woman, whereas I shall then become a poor man."

"But I told you," Cynthia protested. "I...."

"I've always tried to do my duty by you, and I shall continue to do it," Kimber cut in. "That's why I shall view this young man with a careful and a prejudiced eye."

Cynthia got to her feet. She seemed on the point of saying something, then changed her mind and instead hurried from the room, narrowly missing Bensall, who was hovering in the

doorway. Impassively he moved to one side to permit her exit from the room. Then he moved forward as Kimber signalled to him.

"Clear this mess away," Kimber said sourly. "I've lost my appetite."

Bensall began clearing away, using the dinner trolley.

"I don't want to be disturbed," Kimber told him imperiously. "There's a young man, a Mr. Lorrimer, coming. Let him in and then go to bed. Do you understand?"

"Yes, sir."

* * * * * * *

The front door bell rang. Bensall, hovering expectantly, glided across the hallway and opened the door to reveal Peter Lorrimer standing outside.

"Good evening, sir," Bensall murmured.

"Good evening," Peter responded. "Mr. Kimber is expecting me. Mr. Peter Lorrimer."

Bensall nodded. "Very good, sir. If you'd mind waiting a moment, I'll inform him."

Bensall turned and, with a dignified tread, crossed the hallway to Kimber's study. Peter took a few steps forward, and gently closed the door behind him. Then he waited, looking about him.

As he looked up, he saw Cynthia leaning over the banister at the top of the stairs.

"Peter!" she whispered anxiously.

He made a little sign of encouragement. "Don't worry, darling."

Peter turned as Bensall reappeared from the study.

"This way, sir," the servant murmured. He opened the study door, and motioned to Peter to go inside.

"Mr. Lorrimer, sir," Bensall announced.

"Go to bed, Bensall." Kimber glared at his servant dismissively.

"Yes, sir," Bensall assented, imperturbable as ever. Then he withdrew from the room, closing the door carefully behind him,

Kimber fixed his gaze on Peter as he stood just inside the door.

"Come and sit here, Mr. er—Lorrimer."

"Thank you." Peter seated himself on the chair Kimber had indicated.

Kimber continued his an appraising stare, then said: "You want to marry my stepdaughter, Mr. Lorrimer?"

"I do, sir." Peter said levelly.

"How long have you known Cynthia?"

Peter hesitated, then: "About two or three months."

"An unorthodox courting, Mr. Lorrimer. I have only learned of your existence this evening."

Peter moistened his lips. "You see, Mr. Kimber...."

"I do see!" Kimber snapped. "It is only fair to tell you—what you have probably already observed—that my stepdaughter is a very highly-strung girl. Not to put too fine a point on it, she suffers from certain delusions." Kimber paused, studying Peter's rather strained expression.

"Do I appear a very terrifying person to you, Mr. Lorrimer?'

"Well, sir, I...." Peter's voice trailed off uncertainly.

"Do I appear to you to be the kind of person deliberately to make unhappy the only person I have left in the world since my wife's death?"

"I only know what I've been told." Peter said flatly.

Kimber smiled twistedly. "Cynthia, let us face it, suffers from a moderate degree of persecution mania."

"Whatever she suffers from, I'm not going to let her give up her inheritance," Peter said stiffly.

When Kimber spoke again, it was in a complete change of tone. "And when do you propose that this marriage shall take place?"

"As soon as possible." Peter tightened his lips. "I'm taking Cynthia to London tonight."

"Tonight?" The crocodile tears had come back into Kimber's

voice. "You will appreciate this comes as rather a shock to me, Mr. Lorrimer." Kimber made a steeple of his fingers and as he leaned forward, the light caught his diamond ring.

"A great shock," Kimber resumed. "I am a sad and lonely man. It needs thinking about, Mr. Lorrimer...it needs talking about.... Sit back, Mr. Lorrimer. Relax. Ley's talk this over."

* * * * * * *

Cynthia, dressed for travelling, and carrying a suitcase, tiptoed down the stairs, and paused to listen outside Kimber's study door. His voice was faintly audible, but the words were indistinguishable to the anxious girl. Making up her mind suddenly, She crossed to the front door, opened it and went out into the darkness.

* * * * * * *

"...and that was the last that was seen of Cynthia Mason!"

Doctor Morelle permitted himself a sardonic smile as he paused in his dictation to Miss Frayle. "She was not in Lorrimer's car when he went down to the gates at the conclusion of his interview with Samuel Kimber. And although he is reported to have searched for her the whole night through, he found no trace of her. Nor apparently could her stepfather throw any light on her whereabouts. Did she go to London after all? But then, why didn't she communicate with the one friend who was entirely within her confidence—Miss Frayle?"

Miss Frayle, her pencil poised over her notebook, felt a little shiver of pleasure at again being mentioned, and eagerly awaited his next sentence.

But his next words came like a douche of cold water.

"Had Miss Frayle's mental equipment equalled her impetuous anxiety, a great deal of trouble might have been saved. But, alas, that is far from the case...."

Miss Frayle bridled with indignation, but bit her lip.

"...She proceeded to adopt a course of action that can only be described as sheer imbecility."

This was more than even Miss Frayle could stand.

"Dr. Morelle! I must...."

"Quiet, please." Dr. Morelle commanded. "Any interruption disturbs the flow of my thoughts...."

He began to resume his dictation, and as Miss Frayle jabbed viciously at her notebook, she broke the point of her pencil with an audible snap.

Dr. Morelle looked up, frowning. "Take another one!"

Sulkily, Miss Frayle selected another pencil from the container on her desk.

"...Instead of reflecting that the sensible course would have been to consult me immediately," Dr. Morelle resumed, "she decided to play the role of private detective, for which she is so patently ill-equipped, and spend some ten days' leave that was due to her, investigating the fate of Cynthia Mason on the spot. Starting from Paddington Station...."

* * * * * * *

Miss Frayle was clearly in a state of fluster as she emerged from the ticket office at Paddington Station. She had placed her ticket in her mouth, whilst holding her open handbag in one hand and a suitcase in the other.

Jostled by the crowd of people milling about the busy station, she tried vainly without hands to get the ticket out of her mouth into the handbag, In desperation, she put down the suitcase, but just as she was transferring the ticket to the handbag, a hurrying passerby bumped into her, and the contents of the bag were spilled all over the ground.

Quickly diving amongst the hurrying feet, Miss Frayle somehow managed to retrieve her property. Closing the bag, she started to hurry off, having left her suitcase behind. Fortunately she was stopped in the nick of time by an alert fellow traveller, who had been observing her antics with some amusement.

Blushing, Miss Frayle smiled her thanks, and grabbing the suitcase, hurried off towards the platform from which her Great Western Area Express train was shortly to depart.

She had barely settled into her seat when the train began to move off. Ruefully, she reflected that had it not been for the courtesy of one of her fellow travellers, she might well have missed the train. She would, of course, have soon realized that she had left it behind, but in the time taken to retrieve it, her train would have left without her.

Which would undoubtedly have saved both her and Dr. Morelle considerable jeopardy in the days to come. But, as she sat in the speeding train, Miss Frayle's real anxiety over her missing friend's fate obscured any possible appreciation of the difficulties and dangers into which her ill-considered impulse was precipitating her.

It was dusk before Miss Frayle's train reached her destination, a small village a few miles from Barren Tor. She made inquiries of the first local person she saw, and as a result she eventually found herself waiting in a somewhat decrepit shelter waiting for the local bus that would, she was told, take her nearer to her destination.

Darkness was falling by the time the bus stopped at the cottages that marked the last outpost of local civilization.

Miss Frayle was its last passenger, and was about to descend, when the driver, a somewhat taciturn young man, appeared. He helped her with her suitcase.

"Here we are, miss."

"How far is it to Barren Tor from here?"

"Two mile...."

Miss Frayle gave a horrified start. "What—?"

"Two mile," the driver repeated stolidly.

"Can I get a taxi?"

The driver shook his head. "No taxi."

"Isn't there *any* means of transport at all?"

"Sam Price's 'ire car."

"Where's that?" Miss Frayle asked eagerly.

"In the garridge. Big end's gone."

Miss Frayle's face fell. "Then how do I get there?"

The driver shrugged, "Walk."

"But I don't even know the way," Miss Frayle said desperately.

"Straight up the moor road, and past the 'Red Lion'." The bus driver pointed. "Two mile."

"Oh, dear. But...."

"You're not likely to meet no one on the road this time of day. Leastways, unless old Daft Georgie's on the bottle again."

"Daft Georgie?" Miss Frayle faltered

"But 'e don't mean no 'arm, really." The driver moved back to the driving seat of his bus. As he climbed in, he looked back over his shoulder at the disconsolate Miss Frayle, adding: "'E's a bit touched like, you see."

As the bus drove off, Miss Frayle gave a long sigh, then, clutching her suitcase, started up the road. As she went, making the best speed she could, she constantly looked over her shoulder in the fast-fading light.

Night had fallen by the time Miss Frayle, dishevelled and panting, arrived at the gates to the mansion at Barren Tor. Putting down her suitcase, she tried ineffectually to open the gates. As she struggled, she suddenly froze as she thought she heard footsteps behind her. The footsteps drew nearer, and Miss Frayle turned her head bravely to meet her fate.

She saw a grey-haired old man holding a lighted lantern.

"There's a knack to that there," the man said, not unkindly. "Let me show you." He reached across her to release the catch on the gate, as Miss Frayle shrank back.

"What are you frightened of?" he demanded querulously. "Anybody'd think I was Daft Georgie."

"Aren't you Daft Georgie?" Miss Frayle faltered.

The old man looked at her indignantly. "Do I look like him?"

"I'm afraid I don't know what...."

"I'm Old Jim, the village carter."

Miss Frayle breathed an audible sigh of relief.

"I bring his parcels up," Old Jim said.

Miss Frayle alerted. "Mr. Kimber's, you mean?"

"'oo else?" Old Jim frowned. "Not a friend of 'is, are you?"

"Er—no," Miss Frayle said hastily.

Old Jim relaxed. "Then I don't mind telling you...he's the meanest old basket this side of Timbucktoo." His tone became sarcastic. "Yes—nice, cheerful 'ousehold, this is. Old Kimber ready to fly off the handle at the drop of a 'at—old Bensall, the butler, creeping about like twopennorth of lor-luv-us...and now Miss Cynthia's gone."

"Where's she gone to?" Miss Frayle asked hopefully.

The old man shrugged, "Nobody don't seem to know, and nobody don't seem to dare ask questions." He paused, his voice becoming confidential. "But there's something as I can tell you." He leaned across to Miss Frayle and prodded home his points with a podgy forefinger.

"What—what is it?"

"There's a lot of very funny rumours flying about. Lodging as I do at the 'Red Lion' I 'ears lots o' things. There's some as say that Miss Cynthia's better dead nor living in this house. Worked 'er like a slave, 'e did, cos 'e never could keep no female staff, what with 'is tempers. Always trying new housemaids, 'e is—but they never stop. There was a new one supposed to 'ave come this week—but she ain't showed up yet. I imagine she's 'eard about things and isn't 'avin' any."

Old Jim straightened up and stretched himself, then with a gruff "Goodnight," he moved off.

Miss Frayle pulled herself together and set off up the drive.

Reaching the front door, Miss Frayle knocked lightly. After a short interval the door; the door swung slowly open.

Miss Frayle edged inside, looking about her timidly.

She started as a harsh voice suddenly addressed her.

"Who are you? What do you want here?"

Miss Frayle spun round.

The speaker was Kimber, and Miss Frayle saw that he was seated in a wheelchair, Bensall, his manservant, standing along-

side him.

"Well—I—I—I've—er—well...."

Kimber cut short her stammering: "Are you the new house-maid? What's your name? Amy?"

Miss Frayle, with a sudden flash of inspiration, decided to take advantage of Kimber's misapprehension as to her identity.

"Yes...yes!" she assented.

"About time," Kimber said sourly. "Servants seem to think they can do as they like these days. Are you strong? Can you cook? Can you mend clothes? Not afraid of work?"

"N-no, sir." Miss Frayle wilted under the verbal onslaught.

"All right. Bensall will show you to your room."

As Kimber returned to his study, the manservant came forward silently, and picked up Miss Frayle's suitcase. She followed him upstairs until they came to a room, which had formerly been the loft.

Entering after Bensall, Miss Frayle looked around her. It was a somewhat bare, strangely-shaped attic storey.

"It—rambles a bit, doesn't it?" Miss Frayle remarked uneasily.

The manservant nodded, and gave her a sidelong glance. "Very strange house, miss, this. Feller who built it must have been—a little eccentric."

"Er—yes,"

"Down here, miss," Bensall said, and guided her down a short flight of steps leading to a door. He opened it and went inside, Miss Frayle timorously following.

Bensall put down her suitcase and stepped respectfully to one side to allow Miss Frayle to view the room.

In marked contrast to the luxury in Kimber's study, the room was cheaply and dingily furnished with odd and ends of cheap furniture; an iron bedstead, a bamboo table, a pine washstand with a cracked basin. A rickety chair or two, and a chest of drawers, completed the bedroom's meagre furnishings.

Miss Frayle looked round the room with a sinking feeling of dismay. She caught Bensall's eye on her.

"This is your room."

"Thank you, Bensall. "It's—it's lovely."

As the manservant turned to go, Miss Frayle pulled herself together and raised a restraining hand.

She had resolved to begin her detective duties, her mind working furiously to imagine what Dr. Morelle would have done had he been in her shoes. She began to fire questions in a businesslike manner.

"How long have you worked here?"

"Many years now," Bensall replied, somewhat morosely.

"How many are there in the household?"

"Mr. Kimber—me—and you."

A distinct feeling of uneasiness crept over Miss Frayle, but she managed to retain her assumed bravado.

"What about the young lady? Er—someone in the village said there was a—er—a Miss Mason."

"She isn't here any more."

"Oh?" Miss Frayle forced herself to remain casual. "Where's she gone?"

Bensall did not reply. He affected not to have heard the question.

Miss Frayle spoke more loudly, "I said—what's happened to her?"

This time Bensall responded, slowly and reluctantly. His tome was sombre. "Don't ask too many questions. It's much easier here if nobody asks questions." He pointed to the bamboo table. "There's a house telephone over there. Mr. Kimber will call up if he wants you."

Before Miss Frayle could think of voicing the further questions that still chased in her mind, Bensall turned and went out, shutting the door behind him.

Immediately he was gone, Miss Frayle whipped off her hat, and threw it on the bed. Then she went over to the door, and pressed her ear against it. She listened to Bensall's footsteps going away.

Miss Frayle decided to waste no time in continuing her detective work. Opening her handbag, she extracted a pair of gloves,

and put them on.

Carefully opening the door, she crept out, tiptoeing through the shadowy loft.

Reaching a corridor, she proceeded along it until she reached what she took to be a bedroom door. She paused, and looked around her. There was nobody about. Cautiously, she turned the handle on the bedroom door, and found it unlocked. She went inside.

There was sufficient light from an uncurtained window for her to see fairly clearly. She gazed at a luxuriously furnished bedroom, with curtains and furnishings of gay chintz. Obviously—as she had hoped—this was Cynthia's bedroom.

Curiously, she moved slowly around the room, looking for she knew not what. She paused to examine a floral calendar, which had been given pride of place over the dressing table.

She picked it up, and saw an inscription in a sprawling handwriting. She could just make it out:

'To dear Miss Cynthia, with respectful good wishes for a Happy Xmas. Bensall.'

Replacing it carefully, Miss Frayle resumed moving slowly around the room, taking her time.

A second window alcove was curtained off. She moved forward and pulled the curtain aside.

She stifled the shriek that rose to her lips at the sight of a man standing there, staring at her intently.

It was Bensall!

Before she could scream Bensall jumped out from the alcove, grabbing her and covering her mouth with his other hand.

Miss Frayle's eyes revealed her terror. But Bensall's clamped hand across her mouth prevented her from giving voice to her scream.

"Keep quiet and you won't get hurt!" Bensall whispered fiercely. "Nod if you understand."

After a moment's consideration, Miss Frayle nodded, and

Bensall released her, and stood back,

Miss Frayle staggered over to the bedrail, and steadied herself against it.

"What are you doing here?" Bensall demanded, low-voiced.

"I—I—I—well, I...." Miss Frayle was completely at a loss.

"I don't mean in this room," Bensall said. "I mean, *what are you doing in this house?*"

"Housemaid." Miss Frayle gulped.

Bensall's eyes narrowed with disbelief. "With *those* hands? And a genuine new housemaid who knew her job would really call the butler 'Mister'.

"I—I...." Miss Frayle continued to falter helplessly.

"Who *are* you?" Bensall demanded. "The Police?"

Miss Frayle shook her head miserably.

"Have you come about *her*?" Bensall whispered fiercely.

"Who?"

"If he has hurt her...," Bensall began muttering to himself. "If he has hurt her...."

"*He?* You mean Mr....Kimber?"

Bensall looked about him apprehensively. "Ssh!" he hissed.

Miss Frayle was beginning to sense that the man was not her enemy. "Have you asked him about Cynthia?"

"'He' only tells you what he wants you to know." Bensall growled. "You don't ask 'Him' questions."

"She was terrified of him," Miss Frayle told him. "I was her friend and she told me so...and he's got control of all the money—until she gets married."

Bensall gave a grim nod. "I know."

"And this young man she wanted to marry?" Miss Frayle asked.

"Mr. Lorrimer?"

Miss Frayle nodded. "Can't *he* throw any light on what happened?"

Bensall shook his head gloomily. "He's as much in the dark as anyone. He never leaves his cottage now.... I've never seen a man look so strange and ill."

Miss Frayle had a sudden inspiration. "Suppose that's all a bluff?" she suggested. "Suppose Cynthia is hiding there...in his cottage...until she's of age and they can get married without her stepfather's consent?"

Bensall was unimpressed. "If she was there, she'd have let me know."

"But, perhaps she daren't," Miss Frayle persisted. "in case her stepfather found out." She was determined to pursue her theory. "D'you know the way to Mr. Lorrimer's cottage?"

"Certainly," Bensall affirmed.

"Then we'll go and see him now. Both of us." Miss Frayle looked at Bensall appealingly. Judging by that calendar, she reasoned, he must be fond of the girl....

Under her imploring gaze, Bensall wavered, then agreed. "But 'he' mustn't see us leave the house."

"We'll slip out of the back door," Miss Frayle breathed. "Come along."

She moved cautiously towards the door, and Bensall followed her. Suddenly. he turned and gave a low whistle and snapped his fingers.

Miss Frayle looked at him in blank astonishment.

Bensall glanced at her, "You don't mind if I take my little dog, miss? He does so love a walk."

Miss Frayle looked around the room in bewilderment. "Your dog?"

"He'll be no trouble, miss." Bensall; smiled oddly, then as Miss Frayle looked at him in incipient alarm, he added:

"You see, he's dead!"

* * * * * * *

After managing to leave Kimber's house—apparently undetected—Miss Frayke followed Bensall through the night, with a distinct feeling of unease as he occasionally spoke to his invisible dog. She was thankful when at last they came to Peter Lorrimer's cottage.

Bensall approached the front door and knocked heavily.

No answer. Bensall knocked again, but without result.

Miss Frayle expelled a long sigh. "He must be out...." She looked at Bensall. "Should we break in?"

Surprisingly, Bensall promptly agreed. "Leave it to me." He bent down, pulling a tool out of his pocket and inserted it in the lock. A few seconds later there came a distinct click, and the door swung open. As Bensall straightened, Miss Frayle found her courage and entered ahead of him.

The first room they searched was the living room, Bensall switching on the light.

Miss Frayle moved over to a large desk, and began desultorily looking through the papers on it.

Most of them appeared to be the manuscripts of some book Lorrimer was working on, but suddenly Miss Frayle gave an excited exclamation.

"Quick, Bensall, look!"

Bensall hurried across to her side. Miss Frayle brandished one of the documents she had been examining. "It's a will! It's Cynthia's mother's will. I happen to know Cynthia always kept it with her, in case her stepfather destroyed it."

Bensall looked at her keenly. "You mean, Miss Cynthia must have brought it here?"

Before Miss Frayle could answer. There came the sound of a door opening.

Miss Frayle had the presence of mind to quickly put the document back where she had found it before the returning Peter Lorrimer had entered the room.

He paused in astonishment as he saw the two intruders.

"Bensall, what are you doing in here?"

"Well, sir...."

As Bensall prevaricated, Miss Frayle jumped in: "We were taking a walk and we decided to call on you."

Peter looked at her with a frown. "Who are you?"

The intervention had allowed Bensall time to gather his wits. "Begging your pardon, sir, this is the new housemaid at Barren

Tor."

Peter's haggard face became suffused with suspicion. "Mr, Kimber didn't send you to spy on me?"

"Good gracious, no!" Miss Frayle declared.

Peter came into the room, shaking his head. "I wouldn't put anything past him. He's at the bottom of Cynthia's disappearance, you mark my words."

Peter sank wearily into a chair, and rested his forehead on his hand. He remained slumped in the chair, not speaking.

Miss Frayle, who had been expecting a barrage of irate questions as to how they had entered his house, realized that the man had so much on his mind that he appeared to have no concern as to their illegal entry. She stepped forward, determined to tackle Peter about the will.

But just as she was opening her mouth to speak, Bensall again interposed:

"Come along, Amy!"

As Miss Frayle looked at him in astonishment, Bensall took her arm firmly and continued:

"You can see the gentleman clearly doesn't want to be disturbed. We'll call some other time."

Bensall led Miss Frayle from the room, and out of the front door of the cottage. He closed the door carefully, then turned as Miss Frayle touched his shoulder.

"Bensall...listen!" she said eagerly. "Cynthia must have gone to the cottage; otherwise, how could her mother's will have got there?"

Bensall shrugged. "She was there the evening she disappeared, miss—she could have brought it then."

Miss Frayle wrinkled her brow. "Yes, that's true. But what harm would it have done, if I'd told him who I was and asked him about her?"

Bensall took her arm, moving off in the direction of Barren Tor, "I think it best, miss, if, for the moment, we keep your identity secret. Now come on, it's late. We must get back before Mr. Kimber discovers our absence."

* * * * * * *

The next morning found Miss Frayle in the kitchen, trying to maintain her assumed identity as Amy, the hired maid. She was still wearing the stylish visiting dress she had on when she had arrived at Barren Tor, but was seeking to protect it with a large apron.

She was evidently attempting to prepare some kind of egg dish for lunch.

She deposited an armful of ingredients, including a bag of flour, a small bowl of eggs, a jug of milk, and measuring jar on the kitchen table by the side of a huge mixing bowl.

Next, she poured some fat into a large frying pan, standing well back so that it didn't splash her dress. Placing the pan on the stove, she then began to crack eggs into the bowl. To her dismay, the first one fell outside the bowl; the second all the way on to the floor, and whilst she succeeded in getting the third one into the bowl, it had retained half its shell.

"Butter," she muttered to herself, carelessly taking the wrapper from a half-pound packet and tossing it whole into the bowl.

"Flour next...."

She took a large paper bag of flour and began carefully tipping some into the bowl.

Suddenly the fat in the frying pan caught fire.

Alarmed, Miss Frayle spun round, upending the paper bag so that all the flour fell in a deluge all over the table and floor. In desperation, she seized a jug of milk and began pouring it into the frying pan to put out the flame, causing clouds of smoke.

Bensall was watching from the doorway, shaking his head sadly.

Somehow Miss Frayle succeeded in dousing the flame, then she saw Bensall regarding her lugubriously.

She surveyed the mess she had made and smiled at him apologetically.

"I think I'd better start again, don't you?" she said brightly.

Bensall gave a silent nod, watching as Miss Frayle began to gather a new set of ingredients. He was about to say something when there came a harsh shout from somewhere in the distance.

"Bensall!" Kimber was calling irritably. "Bensall!"

Moments later the kitchen door was pushed open, and Kimber entered in his wheelchair. He glared at his manservant.

"Bensall, why hasn't my room been done?"

"Amy's just going up to do it now, sir," Bensall said hastily.

With a snarl Kimber turned to Miss Frayle, who backed away, terrified.

"You lazy little slut! If you don't get down to your work, out you go!" His eyes bulged, and saliva flecked his curling lips. "D'you understand me, you—you—dough-faced dancehall blonde!"

This verbal onslaught was too much even for Miss Frayle, whose terror was overcame by her anger at his words.

"I *won't* be...."

Bensall quickly intervened, grabbing her arm. *"Don't!"* he whispered

"Get upstairs at once!" Kimber shouted. "Do you hear?"

Biting her lip, Miss Frayle hurried out, followed by Bensall.

Kimber looked at the mess on the floor with narrowed eyes, then gripped the wheels of his chair and went out also.

As Miss Frayle entered Kimber's bedroom she was seething with anger. Her usual diffidence had evaporated. She turned her head to look at Bensall, following close behind her.

"How dare he speak to me like that?" she demanded.

"At all costs, don't cross him, miss," Bensall counselled. "There's no knowing what he might do to you in one of his rages."

Miss Frayle hesitated, clenching her fists. Then Bensall's earnest advice had a sobering effect. She turned and began to make the bed, Bensall dexterously assisting.

"He's responsible for Cynthia's disappearance!" Miss Frayle said, breathing hard. "I feel it in my bones he knows all about it. After all, all the money remains in his hands if...."

"Don't say it, miss!" Bensall implored. "It doesn't bear thinking of."

But Miss Frayle had now been struck by another thought. Dropping her side of the blanket, which they were pulling up, and dashed to the wardrobe, she flung it open, disclosing Kimber's suits hanging inside.

Miss Frayle began 'frisking' the pockets of the suits, as Bensall stood watching nervously. "What are you doing?" he asked.

"Searching for a clue...."

"But...what sort of a clue?"

"I don't know," Miss Frayle admitted, continuing her desperate search. "But Dr. Morelle—er—a man I know—says you'll always find clues to where a man has been—in his wardrobe. Bus tickets in a pocket, a woman's hair on a jacket, dust on his shoes...."

Bensall frowned. "Well, you know perfectly well Mr. Kimber hasn't been anywhere. He can't get out of the house except in his chair, and that he hardly ever does."

Miss Frayle was unfazed by this logic. "Never mind. We may find some sort of clue, and—"

She broke off suddenly and pointed to the bottom of the wardrobe.

A row of men's shoes were beautifully cleaned and polished, *except for one pair, which was covered with dust.*

"Look there!" Miss Frayle breathed. "Dust on his shoes!" Her hand flashed down and picked up the dusty pair.

Peering through her thick lenses, she examined the shoes.

"It's ash," she pronounced at length. "And look—" she indicated a suit hanging in the wardrobe—"there's more in the turn-ups of this pair of trousers."

Bensall looked wonderingly. "Ash—and clay."

Miss Frayle furrowed her brows. "But where could it have come from?"

"I don't know, miss," Bensall said slowly. "Perhaps...perhaps from the incinerator in the outhouse...but he can't walk!"

"How do you know?" Miss Frayle demanded. "You mean you haven't *seen* him walk. Come on!"

Bensall looked at her blankly. "Where to?"

"The incinerator, of course—"

She started to move towards the door, but Bensall stopped her.

"We daren't go now, miss, not while *he's* about."

"Then we'll wait until he's gone to bed." Miss Frayle tightened her lips. "Nothing's going to stop me having a look at that incinerator tonight."

* * * * * * *

Two figures were moving furtively in the darkness. They stopped as they reached a narrow, brick-built shed with a door at one end. Dimly discernible in the moonlight was a brick oven against one wall.

The larger of the two figures reached out and pulled open a door, letting in the moonlight, which suffused one end of the shed.

Bensall and Miss Frayle advanced into the shed. Miss Frayle produced a small electric torch from her handbag and flashed it about. She moved over to the oven.

"Someone has been here," she whispered, "the ash has been scattered quite recently."

Bensall bent over the oven. "Look, some turf has been thrown in on top here—it's still green. Perhaps—"

He broke off abruptly at a sudden sound from outside. It was recognizable as approaching footsteps.

Miss Frayle and Bensall stared at each other in horrified silence.

Bensall made a sign to Miss Frayle to switch off her torch, and moved towards the door. At that moment, Miss Frayle, glancing frantically about her, noticed something amongst the ashes. Curiosity overcame her mounting fear and she bent to pick it up. Her hand closed on a sapphire earring. Her torchlight

showed that the setting had been twisted and bent by the heat of the fire. She switched off her torch and crouched by the oven.

Suddenly there was a strangled groan from the door. Miss Frayle looked up.

In the doorway she saw a vague figure grappling with Bensall, silhouetted against the moonlight. The figure lifted an arm and struck downwards viciously.

Bensall gave a strangled groan and fell to the floor. The figure stooped over him for a moment, and then turned away, vanishing into the night.

Miss Frayle, frozen with terror, remained where she was, crouched by the oven. Long seconds passed. When the figure did not return, she pulled herself together and slowly moved towards the doorway.

Bensall was lying motionless where he had fallen. Gingerly Miss Frayle moved past him and looked cautiously out through the door. Seeing no one, she came back and fell to her knees beside Bensall, pillowing his head in her lap.

"Bensall!" she gasped, "Bensall!"

His eyes flickered open.

"Are you badly hurt?"

Bensall groaned.

Miss Frayle bent her head towards him. "Who was it? Did you see?"

Bensall nodded, apparently unable to speak. Miss Frayle noticed that he was clutching at his breast.

Miss Frayle reached down and gently tore his shirt open. Her eyes widened in horror as she saw the extent of his wound. Immediately she tried to staunch the blood with her handkerchief, but she knew instinctively that the wound was a fatal one. She stared at him with tear-filled eyes.

"Who was it? Try to tell me."

Bensall had fixed his glassy eyes on the ground by his side. Slowly his hand made a soft, caressing gesture.

"Little dog...look after...little dog."

"Yes, yes, I will!" Miss Frayle promised. "But tell me, who

was it? Try to tell me."

But Bensall made no answer. He suddenly became rigid; then his head fell to one side.

With a shudder of horror, Miss Frayle gently lowered him to the ground. She rose to her feet, and cautiously went out. But in doing so, she was unaware that she had dropped her blood-soaked handkerchief.

Somehow Miss Frayle managed to make her way back to the house. She had barely reached the back door, which they had left on a latch, when there was a vivid flash of lightning, followed by a low rumbling. A storm was breaking.

Risking her torch in short bursts, Miss Frayle made her way on tiptoe through the house, Reaching the hall telephone, she lifted the instrument with a trembling hand, and dialled for the Operator.

"I want a call to London, please," she whispered. "It's urgent.... Welbeck 74382 Reverse the charges...."

* * * * * * *

Doctor Morelle was at home, in his shirtsleeves, practising fencing thrusts in a long mirror, when his telephone rang.

With a deep sigh, he dropped his foil and went to his desk and picked up the telephone.

"Dr. Morelle speaking...will I accept a reversed charges call from where? I've never heard of it. Where is it?... Devonshire. I'm sorry. I know nobody in that vicinity. I do not accept the call...what name?...Frayle? I see, in that case, very well, but for three minutes only. Hello...."

When she heard the Doctor's voice Miss Frayle was almost hysterical with relief at having made contact, Desperately she restrained herself from almost shouting into the receiver.

"Oh, Dr. Morelle...! It's me...Miss Frayle.... I'm in terrible trouble.... I found Cynthia...but she's dead...."

With an expression of annoyance Dr. Morelle held the receiver away from his ear. The metallic sound of Miss Frayle's

voice as she babbled on hysterically was clearly audible in the room.

"I found her earring...in a brick oven and Bensall, the butler, has been murdered...only a few minutes ago. We found ashes on his boots...he was kind...now I'm alone...."

Dr. Morelle broke in, his voice stern with exasperation: "Miss Frayle! I insist you remain silent for the space of a minute...."

Miss Frayle had been conditioned by her long association with Dr. Morelle: the habit of obedience caused her to instantly remain silent, her mouth open as she listened to the doctor's sardonic voice.

"...and breathe in deeply through the nose, expelling through the mouth...."

Obediently, Miss Frayle proceeded to breathe in through her nose and gasp out through her mouth.

Dr. Morelle gave a sidelong glance at his fencing foil.

"It's bad enough to be distracted from my work, which is of—er—considerable scientific importance...but when it's to listen to some monstrous verbal phantasmagoria of charred bones, ashes on boots, and murdered butlers...."

His biting sarcasm was too much, even for Miss Frayle. She interrupted with weary earnestness:

"There's no time for all that stuff, Dr. Morelle. I'm desperate. Five minutes ago a man died in my arms.... I'm in danger myself...real danger...you've just *got* to come and help me."

At that instant Dr. Morelle realized that his secretary was being serious, and his manner changed to matter-of-fact prac-ticality.

"Very well, Miss Frayle, I'll come by the midnight train, provided you do exactly as I tell you."

"Yes, Dr. Morelle."

"Write me a report of everything that's happened. Omit nothing, and embroider nothing. What is the nearest station to Barren Tor?"

"Moorminster," Miss Frayle panted. "It's three miles."

"Have you anyone you could send there with your report?"

Miss Frayle furrowed her brow, then suddenly had a flash of inspiration. "Yes—Old Jim! I can find him at the 'Red Lion'."

"Good. Have him hand your manuscript—sealed, of course—to the stationmaster. I will collect it from him tomorrow morning and take whatever course I feel to be the most advisable under the circumstances. When you've finished handing over your report, go back to the house and go straight back to bed, and try and get some sleep. Try not to do anything stupid."

Miss Frayle gave a gasp of dismay. "Do I *have* to return here, Doctor?"

"Yes. It is essential to my investigation that your—er—employer does not suspect anything."

"But—" Miss Frayle protested faintly.

"In the event of criminal activity, which immediately threatens your own personal safety, communicate with the local Police Constabulary...or preferably lock your bedroom door... goodbye!"

Miss Frayle carefully replaced the receiver, and steeled herself for further efforts.

* * * * * * *

Miss Frayle closed and locked her bedroom door. A lightning flash lighted up the room. She gave a little shudder, thankful for the fact that the storm had abated during her journey to and back from the 'Red Lion'. But now it was starting up again.

As the thunder rumbled she wedged the door with a chair, and then proceeded to drag more furniture in the room against the door, making a barricade.

She breathed a sigh of relief, feeling that now she was adequately protected from Kimber.

As an afterthought she looked under the bed. Nothing there. She relaxed a little, looked again at the furniture barricade, and drew solace from it.

Miss Frayle gave a start as the telephone rang suddenly.

She put out her hand, and hesitated, lacking the courage to

lift the receiver. Then, as it continued to ring, she jerked up the receiver.

"Hello?" she whispered.

"Are you there?" Kimber's voice demanded.

"I'm perfectly all right. I'm very well, thank you."

"Stop talking nonsense and listen," Kimber snapped impatiently. "You had better be up sharp in the morning. Bensall has left...."

As Miss Frayle replaced the telephone, she felt a chill of fear. Bensall left? *How did Kimber know?*

A sudden loud clap of thunder sent her scurrying to the bed, where she covered herself with the bedclothes,

* * * * * * *

Dr. Morelle reached out a lean hand, and knocked authoritatively on the front door of Kimber's mansion.

It was a fine winter's day, and still early morning.

He was about to knock again, when the door half opened. Miss Frayle peered cautiously out, then, seeing who it was, she flung the door wide open. Her face beamed at him in relief and thankfulness.

Dr. Morelle placed a warning finger to his lips, then spoke in a low tone:

"Though flattered at my reception, it is essential you should pretend you don't know who I am from Adam. In other words, Miss Frayle, to use a distressing colloquialism, preserve the 'poker face', or, which should come naturally to you, the 'dead pan'."

Miss Frayle was still euphoric. "You don't know how much it means to see you—!"

Dr. Morelle waved a hand to cut her short. "I've read your report—it's very interesting." He looked at her and frowned. "You look as if you didn't sleep well."

"Oh, Doctor Morelle, I didn't. I was alone in the house with him last night"—she jerked a thumb over her shoulder to indi-

cate Kimber—"I had all the furniture stacked against the door."

With a nod of his head Dr. Morelle indicated that he wished to enter, He moved past her into the hall.

As Miss Frayle closed the door behind him, Dr. Morelle said loudly, "Will you kindly inform your employer that Professor Harper would appreciate the privilege of a few words with him? My card."

He presented his card to Miss Frayle, who boggled for a moment, but pulled herself together quickly.

"Yes, sir. I'll tell him." She moved off, leaving Dr. Morelle standing in the hallway. Going to the door of Kimber's study, she knocked and entered.

Directly he was alone, Dr. Morelle made a rapid examination of the hall. He was just looking at the ferrule of a heavy walking stick which he had found leaning against the wall, when the door of the study opened, and Miss Frayle came out.

Immediately Dr. Morelle caught her by the arm and drew her aside. Leaning towards her he whispered urgently:

"Now pay attention. After I have been with Kimber a few minutes, come in with some news of a domestic crisis, that will make him come out with you for a minute or two, leaving me alone in there."

Miss Frayle gulped and nodded vigorously. She pushed open the door of Kimber's study, and started to announce him:

"Doctor Mo—"

"*Professor* Harper," Dr. Morelle cut in quickly. "So kind of you to spare me a few moments, Mr. Kimber."

He swept into the room past Miss Frayle as she remained frozen, figuratively biting her tongue off.

Kimber was sitting at his desk. On his left hand he was still wearing the heavy diamond ring as on the night of Peter Lorrimer's visit. Dr. Morelle noticed it as it glinted, and he saw too that the curtains were dawn over the windows, the room being lit by a strong desk-light.

Kimber came forward in his chair to meet Dr. Morelle.

Kimber had noticed the doctor's glance to the drawn curtains.

"Please forgive this somewhat bizarre lighting, but I've got into the habit of working by artificial light."

"How interesting," Dr. Morelle murmured. "And how conducive to concentration."

"Sit down, Professor," Kimber invited. "What can I do for you?"

Dr. Morelle seated himself opposite to Kimber, occupying the same chair that Peter Lorrimer had sat in on the fateful night that Cynthia had disappeared.

"Briefly, my mission is this," Dr. Morelle began his prepared story. "I have been invited by the County Historical and Topographical Society to prepare a paper on the old houses of the district. I wondered if you would be kind enough to give me some information about Barren Tor."

"A reasonably full account of the house and its historical associations can be found in Riddal's *Antiquities of Devon*—a work you doubtless know," Kimber said.

"I do indeed, but its date of publication was 1827," Dr. Morelle came back smoothly. "I am sure there must be a great deal of interesting material of more recent date."

Kimber shook his head. "Virtually none, I assure you." As he spoke, Kimber cupped his chin in his hands in a characteristic attitude, and Dr. Morelle noticed his diamond ring catching the light.

"Riddal writes of some particularly fine carved panelling in the best bedroom," Dr. Morelle went on. "I would be very grateful for an opportunity of examining it."

"I have neither the time nor the money to keep this house in the state of preservation it warrants," Kimber said flatly.

Dr. Morelle smiled thinly. "Has anybody any money these days, Mr. Kimber?"

Kimber was watching Dr. Morelle closely. He leaned forward, his eyes shining in the light of the desk lamp. He turned the diamond ring round and round on his finger so that its facets kept catching the light.

"To a philosopher, money is immaterial," he murmured.

"Yet even philosophers must eat, Mr. Kimber."

Kimber leaned forward, staring directly into Dr. Morelle's eyes. "It is surprising how little food they need, Professor. What a philosopher needs is—relaxation. To relax! That is the answer to the stress of modern life. Look at you! Tense and on edge! Relax, Professor, relax, and you will find...."

At that moment the door was flung open and Miss Frayle rushed in, in an assumed panic.

"Oh, sir! Do please come at once! The boiler's bursting, sir. Steam is coming out, and it's boiling over and.... Oh, sir! Do come, sir!"

She almost dragged a visibly annoyed Kimber from the room. Left alone, Dr. Morelle leapt into action. Going first to Kimber's desk, he pulled out each drawer, getting a quick idea of the contents. Once he gave a grunt of satisfaction, and paused to note down an address.

Next he moved swiftly along the bookshelves, glancing at the titles. He paused at one section with evident interest, muttering to himself in a pleased fashion. "Really! Most interesting!" he muttered. "Most interesting!"

He was standing in the middle of the room when he door was flung open and a very angry Kimber came back in.

"That girl's a fool!" he spat. "I'll have to get rid of her. Nothing the matter with the boiler at all." With a visible effort, he managed to control his temper. He turned to Dr. Morelle.

"Well Professor, I don't think we have anything more to say to each other."

Dr. Morelle shrugged amiably; he had accomplished his mission.

"No, I must be on my way. I've suddenly remembered a pressing appointment."

Kimber glared at him suspiciously. "What is it?"

Dr. Morelle gave a sardonic smile as he turned to the door.

"Not being a philosopher—lunch! Good day, Mr. Kimber."

He went out into the hallway, leaving a thoroughly puzzled man staring after him.

Leaving the house, Dr. Morelle walked briskly down the drive. He hesitated as there was a sudden rustling in the bushes, and Miss Frayle cautiously poked her head out, her hair all awry.

Dr. Morelle stopped, ostensibly to light a cigarette.

"I'm going now to see Mr. Lorrimer—wait for me in the house," he instructed Miss Frayle tersely. Then he smiled faintly. "By the way, that was really quite ingenious, that boiler device. You used your brains for once. Quite surprising!"

Having delivered this surprising comment, he threw away the match and walked on.

Miss Frayle gazed after him with a tender smile after this generous and unexpected compliment.

* * * * * * *

Dr. Morelle entered the gardens surrounding Peter Lorrimer's cottage, striding purposely to the front door, where he knocked.

At length Peter Lorrimer opened the door, Dr. Morelle noted with professional interest that the man's face was haggard with worry. He glared at his unwanted visitor.

"Go away, I'm busy. If it's money you want, I haven't got any."

Dr. Morelle smiled reassuringly. "The financial implications of the matter I wish to discuss with you are entirely to your advantage. I wish to offer you some employment—in a literary capacity."

Peter hesitated, then decided to let Dr. Morelle come in. Once he was inside, he closed the door quickly.

Dr. Morelle followed Peter into his living room. The haggard man did not invite him to be seated;

"Well?" he demanded bluntly.

Dr. Morelle assumed a breezy military bearing. "My name is Welton, Captain Roger Welton. I'm starting a publishing firm in Exeter. I want someone to write a guidebook for me—light amusing stuff, you know. Your name was given to me."

"Oh?" Peter spoke listlessly.

"You look ill," Dr. Morelle told him frankly. "What's the matter with you?"

"Nothing...nothing," Peter muttered. "I'm all right."

However, the man certainly didn't look all right. To Dr. Morelle's professional gaze, he was behaving in the manner of a very sick man, and his declaration was totally unconvincing.

"You don't *look* all right," Dr. Morelle pursued. "Have you seen a doctor?"

"What good are doctors?"

"I should go all the same," Dr. Morelle told him. "A doctor or a psychiatrist. Nerve strain can play havoc with the healthiest of men."

Peter looked at him sharply

"Who said anything about nerve strain?"

"Perhaps something has gone wrong with your plot?" Dr. Morelle suggested.

"Plot?"

"Of your latest story, I mean," Dr. Morelle said smoothly. "Whatever it is, there is only one cure—relaxation."

As he spoke, a shaft of sunlight was shining through the window directly on to his face, causing his eyes to gleam and glisten. He unbuttoned his coat, revealing that he had a monocle hanging against his waistcoat on a black silk thread. As he spoke, he held the thread in his fingers so that the monocle began to swing gently to and fro, so that it too winked and glistened in the sunshine.

"That is the secret for overtaxed nerves," Dr. Morelle murmured. "Relax! Empty your brain of all thought...allow all your resistance to subside...as it were anaesthetize your will."

Peter began to become irritated, and blinked heavily. "For heaven's sake, don't fiddle with that eyeglass!"

Dr. Morelle dropped the eyeglass and changed his tone. "I must apologise for sermonising when I really came to see you on business."

Peter frowned. "Can't we discuss it some other time?"

"It won't take a minute," Dr. Morelle said quickly.

Somewhat reluctantly, Peter seated himself at his desk, and Dr. Morelle dropped into a nearby chair.

"Let me tell you about it. It's a pocket guide with a new twist to it...."

He picked up his despatch case and unstrapped it while continuing his sales talk:

"...we arrange with all the hotel keepers in the district to let us have weekly a list of guests. Then we mail each of them a copy, and that gives us the circulation to attract the advertising on which we live. Of course it has to be well written, just in case anyone starts reading it! Let me show you the sort of make-up we have in mind."

Dr. Morelle now extracted from his case a small booklet and put the case on the desk. However, in doing so he successfully contrived to knock the large pile of papers on to the floor. With profuse apologies, he leapt up and started to pick the papers

"Oh, how very careless of me. Don't move, please! I'll pick them up. I do hope they weren't in any particular order."

Dr. Morelle's purposefully questing hands picked up the will, which Miss Frayle had found on her visit, together with another paper of similar size, and a document which looked like a Registration Certificate.

Scowling, Peter snatched the papers out of Dr. Morelle's hands and thrust them into a drawer. "Leave them alone, please. *I'll* pick them up."

He hurriedly collected the rest of the papers and also put them into a drawer.

"Now, about this little pocket guidebook...," Dr. Morelle began.

"I'm not interested," Peter snapped.

Dr. Morelle made another attempt. "Can't I persuade you to change your mind? We propose to develop it into something big, you know. The money may not be large for the first job but—mighty oaks from little acorns grow, what?"

"I'm sorry, I haven't time."

"Oh, I see. You're already making good money with your

books and short stories. Is that it?"

"Yes," Peter snapped.

Dr. Morelle rose. "Lucky man! Young, unencumbered and as one might say, *the sole beneficiary.*"

Peter gave a start. "What?"

"From the proceeds of your work, of course!" Dr. Morelle said blandly. "Good day. Don't worry. I'll see myself out."

Dr. Morelle walked briskly away from the cottage. He had not gone very far, however, before he stopped. Pulling out his notebook he jotted down a few words. He looked at his watch, and moved off down the road.

After a few minutes he came to a telephone box, and went inside.

He inserted coins in the box, and consulted a pencilled list of the calls he proposed to make.

"Messrs. Biddle & Rumble, Solicitors.... Scotland Yard...all local Registry offices...," he muttered to himself, tapping impatiently at the receiver rest. "Miss Frayle should be doing this detail work!"

* * * * * * *

The door to the incinerator in the grounds of Kimber's property opened, letting in a bright shaft of sunlight, A man's figure appeared, unrecognisable when silhouetted against the bright light. Entering quickly, he closed the door behind him.

Darkness closed in, until the man switched on an electric torch, swinging the beam round the shed as the man searched for something. He froze as he heard the noise of the latch of the door being raised behind him. He immediately switched off the torch, and darkness descended again.

The door slowly opened, once more admitting Miss Frayle.

She came into the shed gingerly, leaving the door open, and expecting to find the body of Bensall.

Her eyes widened in horrified surprise when she saw that the body was no longer there. She stood for a moment in indecision,

and then started searching for something on the ground.

Further into the shed, the man who had entered earlier stood motionless in the shadow of the oven.

Miss Frayle, her head bent as she continued to search on the ground, slowly came nearer to him. She carried straight on until her head bumped into the stationary figure.

At once she looked up, let out a piercing scream, and jumped back, edging back into the sunlight.

She was about to scream again when the man slipped out of the shadows—and revealed himself to be none other than Dr. Morelle.

"Please, Miss Frayle, try and refrain from screaming in that discordant manner."

Miss Frayle's relief was palpable. "Oh, what a shock you gave me!"

"You could have avoided it if you'd waited at Barren Tor as I told you," Dr. Morelle admonished.

"I suppose I shouldn't have come really...." She broke off and again looked round. "But I suddenly remembered that I'd dropped something." Failing to find what she was looking for, she looked up at Dr. Morelle, who was watching her performance with controlled impatience.

"But, Dr. Morelle, I don't understand this. Bensall's gone! And he was lying there!"

"His body was removed by the murderer," Dr. Morelle said calmly. "That was only to be expected."

"Then surely we oughtn't to be walking about in here. There may be footprints...." She paused, then added brightly, "We could take plaster casts."

"By a regrettable oversight I omitted to fill my pockets with plaster," Dr. Morelle said dryly. "And now may I ask what has brought you here? What are you searching for?"

"I suddenly remembered that I'd dropped my handkerchief here last night," Miss Frayle replied worriedly.

"Your handkerchief?"

"Miss Frayle nodded, "Yes, I used it for poor Bensall's

wound—tried to stop the blood...."

"Was it a small one?" Dr. Morelle interrupted sharply. "Obviously a woman's handkerchief?"

Miss Frayle gave him a puzzled glance. "Yes. But...."

Dr. Morelle frowned. "You haven't found it?"

Miss Frayle looked about her. "No. It should have been lying just there." She pointed to the middle of the floor near the door.

Dr. Morelle gripped her firmly but gently by the arm as he spoke levelly:

"You realize, Miss Frayle, the implication?"

"No!" Miss Frayle looked her puzzlement.

"The absence of the handkerchief," Dr. Morelle said heavily, "proves that Bensall's murderer found it when he removed the body."

"That's Kimber," Miss Frayle said emphatically. "He knew about Bensall last night...said he'd sent him away...it *must* be him!"

"What I'm trying to emphasize to you, Miss Frayle," Dr. Morelle said patiently, "is not the identity of the murderer, but the fact that you are in the greatest personal danger."

"*I* am?" Miss Frayle asked blankly.

"Now that the murderer knows you were here at the actual time of the murder, he has only one course open to him."

"What's that?" Miss Frayle stammered nervously.

"To murder you. Miss Frayle!"

Miss Frayle gave a strangled gasp of terror and turned in a panic, making for the door.

Anticipating her move, Dr. Morelle strode forward quickly and again grabbed her by the arm. She swung to face him, her lips trembling.

"That's why I'm not going to let you out of my sight till I've cleared everything up."

Miss Frayle calmed, and gave a little shudder.

"I'll accompany you back to the house, via the back entrance. Kimber's penchant for keeping his study curtained will aid us considerably."

* * * * * * *

Miss Frayle paced up and down her bedroom with a distinctly worried expression. In total contrast, Dr. Morelle sprawled lazily in a chair by the fire, apparently at peace with the world. He looked up and regarded her with disdain.

"My dear Miss Frayle, I would be greatly obliged if you would kindly settle somewhere. I find your persistent leaping about the room, like a startled goat, most disturbing."

"It's all right for you, Dr. Morelle!" Miss Frayle was indignant. "You're not likely to be murdered any minute."

Dr. Morelle smiled faintly. "I always feel a most profound pity for those whose intellectual attainment does not provide a philosophy to cover such a contingency. There is a chance, as you say, that you may be struck down this evening—if my plans for your protection should prove inadequate. Very well, but you take rather similar chances every moment of every day. For all you know, the ceiling above your head may be structurally unsound and fall on you this very instant."

Instinctively Miss Frayle looked up and ducked involuntarily.

"That nail file," Dr. Morelle resumed, "with which you are fidgetting may, at this moment, be depositing some fatal virus in some indiscernible puncture in your epidermis...."

Thoroughly alarmed, Miss Frayle hurled the nail file from her, on to the dressing table.

Doctor Morelle continued relentlessly: "...tomorrow, you will have to cross a road...."

"Dr. Morelle—please!"

Doctor Morelle regarded her with an air of pained surprise, which was not entirely convincing. "I am merely endeavouring, my dear Miss Frayle, to give you a comforting philosophy."

Miss Frayle looked pained. "If that's your idea of a—" She broke off abruptly as the telephone rang. "Kimber!" she exclaimed, glancing at Dr. Morelle in indecision.

"Answer it," he instructed calmly.

"What are you doing?" Kimber's voice came over the line.

"Oh— Ch-changing, sir," Miss Frayle faltered.

"Get to the kitchen at once, and get on with supper," Kimber instructed harshly. "For two, Mr. Lorrimer's coming."

"V-very good, sir."

Dr. Morelle, who had been able to overhear Kimber's barked instructions, smiled complacently.

"And," Kimber added, "I want the sherry and two glasses put in the study."

"Yes, sir."

As Miss Frayle hung up, Dr. Morelle jumped up from his chair. "And now to work!"

Going over to the door, he very quietly unlocked it. Then he opened it gingerly and looked out into the corridor. On seeing that the coast was clear, he turned to Miss Frayle.

"Directly I'm outside, lock the door again."

"But. Dr. Morelle...."

"Lock the door and stay here till I send for you. Do as I say."

He slipped out into the passage, closing the door behind him.

Miss Frayle hesitated for a moment, and then locked the door as she had been instructed.

* * * * * * *

Seen from the outside, Kimber's mansion was in darkness, except for a light in the hall, which threw a dim glow over the drive before the front door.

Peter Lorrimer stood for a moment surveying the house, then he moved towards the back of it.

* * * * * * *

In her bedroom, Miss Frayle wandered over to the mantelpiece. Evidently still restless, she looked at the clock. Her lips tightened as she came to a decision. Turning, she went over to the door and unlocked it.

She opened it just a few inches and listened. All was quiet.

Making up her mind not to wait any longer, she pulled the door wide enough to slip out, putting her hand to the light switch.

Miss Frayle tiptoed along the corridor towards the stairs. She paused and listened. All was still quiet. The light was on in the hall. Slowly she started to go down the stairs.

Miss Frayle was halfway down the stairs when there suddenly sounded a loud and eerie screeching wail. She was so startled she nearly fell, but managed to save herself by clutching at the banister.

As the eerie wail was repeated, she looked about her desperately, but saw nothing to account for the sound.

Heaving a sigh of relief she continued down the stairs. Reaching Kimber's study, she listened outside for a moment, but heard nothing. She was just straightening when she was grabbed from behind, and a hand clamped brutally over her mouth.

* * * * * * *

Kimber propelled himself into the hall in his wheel chair. Closing the front door, he proceeded to enter his study.

The only light in the curtained room came from the desk lamp, and seated at the desk, calmly smoking, was Dr. Morelle.

Kimber stared in disbelief. "What the hell—!" he exploded.

"Come in, Mr. Kimber," Dr. Morelle said pleasantly, "come in."

Kimber propelled his wheelchair up to the desk. Judging by his angry expression, he was working himself up into one of his towering rages.

"Relax. Mr. Kimber," Dr. Morelle said calmly. "I've been waiting for a chat with you."

Kimber flushed angrily. "May I ask, Professor Harper...?"

"No, Mr. Kimber," Dr. Morelle interrupted blandly. "That was, I'm ashamed to say, somewhat wide of the truth. Actually, my name is Morelle, Dr. Morelle."

He paused, awaiting a reaction from Kimber, who only

frowned in bewilderment.

"Dr. Morelle?"

"D'you mean to say that name doesn't mean anything to you?"

"Nothing at all!" Kimber snapped. "Now, will you kindly explain to me how you got into my house, and what you think you're doing here!"

"I told you, I wanted a further chat with you."

Kimber narrowed his eyes. "What about?"

"The murder of your stepdaughter, Mr. Kimber!"

The unexpectedness of this verbal attack appeared to take the wind out of Kimber's sails. He slumped in his chair, staring open-mouthed at his visitor.

Dr. Morelle leaned forward so that the light of the desk lamp shone directly on his face. At the same time he started to swing his eyeglass to and fro so that it kept catching and reflecting the light.

"A matter on which I think you can throw a great deal of light."

Kimber licked his lips and tried to pull himself together. But his eyes kept following the swing of the flashing eyeglass.

"I don't know what you're talking about. Who led you to believe my stepdaughter was murdered?"

Dr. Morelle kept staring intently at Kimber, and steadily swinging his eyeglass, which consistently riveted Kimber's gaze.

"You did, Mr. Kimber."

"Nonsense. She's just—gone away."

"Where to?" Dr. Morelle asked sharply.

"I don't know. And anyway, it's no business of yours."

"Possibly she went away—with Bensall. He's away too, isn't he?"

Kimber squirmed in his chair, but his eyes were still held by the swinging eyeglass.

"You'd prefer her to be with Bensall rather than—Peter Lorrimer?" Dr. Morelle suggested.

"Why should I mind if she were with Peter Lorrimer?"

"Because he'd insist on your paying over her inheritance. Mr. Kimber."

Kimber made one final effort to regain control of the situation, Straightening up, he shouted: "Why should I answer your questions? Get out of my house. Get out—!"

Dr. Morelle leaned over the desk, catching Kimber by his shoulder, and forcing him back into his chair.

"Sit back, Mr. Kimber, and relax!"

From where Kimber sat, he could see Dr. Morelle's eyes flashing in the light, while the eyeglass seemed to glisten more brightly every rime it swung back and forth...back and forth....

"That was what you said to me, wasn't it? Relax, you said... surrender your will, you said. And now it's the other way round, Mr. Kimber, and I'm going to succeed where you failed...."

Kimber was now making a terrific effort to resist Dr. Morelle's hypnosis. But he could not control his eyes, nor indeed now his whole head, which were moving to and fro in time to the swinging eyeglass.

"...Because, you see," Dr. Morelle murmured, "I happen be a professional in hypnotism, while you are only an amateur."

Suddenly Kimber's resistance collapsed. His eyes became fixed and glassy, and he slumped back in his chair.

Dr. Morelle rose from behind the desk he had been leaning across, and came round to look at Kimber. He flipped his fingers under his eyes and grunted with satisfaction when they did not blink. Turning to the windows he called out:

"All right, Inspector!"

From behind the heavy curtains that hid the windows stepped a police Inspector accompanied by his Detective-Sergeant. Both men were in plain clothes.

The came forward and wonderingly looked at Kimber, who continued to sit slumped in his chair, staring straight before him.

Inspector Harris glanced at Dr. Morelle, "He's really in a hypnotic trance?"

"Try and wake him up," Dr. Morelle invited, dryly.

Inspector Harris shook Kimber vigorously. "Mr. Kimber! Mr. Kimber!"

But Kimber did not come round, remained unmoving, staring before him.

The Inspector turned back to Dr. Morelle. "You've put him under all right. But how's that going to help us?"

"He'll answer any questions I ask him—and truthfully."

Harris frowned. "I doubt if we can use any statements made while he's in this condition.

"I'm not suggesting you should," Dr. Morelle said smoothly. "But when he has told us the true story—I emphasise, his *true* story, as he believes it, then I'll waken him, and you can caution him and question him in the ordinary way."

As Inspector Harris still looked doubtful, Dr. Morelle added: "Frankly, Inspector, I'm not interested in the legal aspect of this case. All I am concerned with is arriving at the truth. How you deal with the truth when you've heard it is entirely your affair."

The Inspector nodded. "Very good, Dr. Morelle. Carry on in your own way."

Dr. Morelle once more sat down in the chair under the lamp. Gently but firmly he addressed Kimber directly:

"Mr. Kimber, can you hear me?"

"Yes." Kimber's voice was toneless.

"You will answer my questions with absolute truthfulness?"

"Yes...."

* * * * * * *

The outer door of the hut containing the incinerator was closed, but the place was lit by the glow of the fire coming from the open oven doors. A man was standing by them, feeding the fire with lumps of peat and logs of wood.

The man straightened up and turned, looking across the room to where Miss Frayle was lying against the wall. Her hands were tied behind her back, and a handkerchief was tied across her mouth, acting as an effective gag.

Her eyes revealed that she was in an extremity of terror, as she watched Peter Lorrimer stoking the fire....

* * * * * * *

In Kimber's study, watched by the two policemen, Dr. Morelle began his interrogation.

"Why did you keep your stepdaughter virtually a prisoner in this house? Was it so that she would have no opportunity of getting married?"

"Yes," Kimber assented tonelessly.

"Why did you oppose her marriage? Was it because in that event all the money passed to her under her mother's will?"

"Yes."

"When she told you she wished to marry Peter Lorrimer, what action did you take?" Dr. Morelle asked shrewdly.

Kimber's eyes were glazed and expressionless, and his voice gentle and matter-of-fact as he answered:

"I decided she must die."

"How did you plan to kill her?"

"I hypnotised Peter Lorrimer, and when he was under my influence ordered him to kill her, and destroy the remains in the incinerator."

"And then?" Dr. Morelle prompted.

"After a suitable time, I planned to pass over sufficient evidence to the police for Lorrimer to be convicted of her murder."

"And Bensall?"

"He was getting suspicious."

"And the housemaid—Amy? Have you any plans for her?"

"Lorrimer is dealing with her now," Kimber said emotion-lessly.

At this chilling revelation Inspector Harris stepped forward anxiously, but Dr. Morelle waved him back. "Don't worry," he reassured him. "I have taken the necessary precautions. My assistant, Miss Frayle, alias Amy, is locked in her room, waiting

to be sent for."

Inspector Harris was still concerned. "But what I don't understand is, surely Lorrimer must realise...."

Dr. Morelle shook his head. "It is a proven fact, Inspector, that the victim of an hypnotic trance has no memory of anything that occurred during that trance." He glanced at his watch. "Lorrimer should be here any moment now. I suggest that while we're waiting for him, I get Miss Frayle down, so that when I recall Kimber from his trance, all the principals that remain will be present."

"Very well."

"Perhaps Detective-Sergeant Jackson wouldn't mind fetching her?" Dr. Morelle suggested.

"Certainly, sir," Jackson assented. "Which room is she in?"

"Right at the top of the house—through the loft."

"Very good, sir." Jackson turned to go.

"Should she seem reluctant to unlock the door," Dr. Morelle added pompously, "just assure her that it is *I* who have sent for her."

"Yes, sir,"

As Jackson left the room, Dr. Morelle turned to the Inspector. "Miss Frayle has a genius for doing the right thing at the wrong moment—which is only exceeded by her capacity for doing the wrong thing at the right moment."

"Er—quite." The Inspector looked nonplussed for a moment, then moved on to a point that had been puzzling him. "Tell me, Dr. Morelle, what put you on to Kimber's hypnotism stunt?"

Dr. Morelle smiled thinly. "The poor deluded man actually had the effrontery to try his skill on me! Then I took a glance at those books"—he waved a hand to the wall bookshelves—"practically every book that's ever been written on the subject of hypnotism is on those shelves. I at once realized that the man was a self-taught amateur."

At that moment he door opened and Jackson came hurrying back—alone.

"Excuse me, sir, but there's no one in that room."

For once, Dr. Morelle was completely nonplussed. "No one there?" he said slowly.

"The door isn't locked either," Jackson went on. "I looked in. The room's empty."

Dr. Morelle realized what had happened. Frowning, he said: "As usual, she must have disobeyed instructions. The crass little idiot! And with Lorrimer about!"

He raced across the room to the door, calling to the two policemen as he went: "Come along, both of you!"

Inspector Harris hesitated, pointing to Kimber. "But what about him?"

Dr. Morelle looked back at him from the doorway. "He won't move till I release him. Now, come along with me!"

The two men followed him out of the study. "There's the kitchen, Inspector." Dr. Morelle pointed to it across the hall. "Have a look in there, will you?"

As the Inspector hurried to the kitchen door while Dr. Morelle, followed by Jackson, rushed up the stairs. Reaching the top, they hurried along the corridor to the door of Miss Frayle's room.

Dr. Morelle flung open the door and switched on the light. Striding into it he saw that the room was indeed empty. Meanwhile, Jackson was examining the lock.

"Key's on the inside, sir. There's no sign of the lock being tampered with."

For once in his life, Dr. Morelle was really perturbed. When he spoke, his somewhat pompous manner had temporarily vanished.

"It's as I feared. That girl's sheer bone from the neck up!" Noticing that the curtains were not drawn, he crossed to the window and examined it rapidly to see if anyone could have climbed in. The window was firmly closed. He looked back at Jackson as he stood by the door. "Let's get back downstairs."

Jackson switched off the light and went out. Dr. Morelle strode across the darkened room to join him, then paused as, out of the corner of his eye, he noticed a flickering red glow

reflected in the dressing table mirror.

Quickly he spun round and hurried to the window and looked out. Above the trees at one point was a dull red glow, getting brighter. As he looked a thick spiral of smoke rose up.

"My God! That's the incinerator!" Turning, he plunged after Jackson.

"Quick! Find the Inspector—make for the back door! We've got to get to the incinerator outside. There's just a chance—if we hurry!"

* * * * * * *

Peter Lorrimer turned back to the fire and checked that it was burning fiercely. Then he crossed to the bound figure of Miss Frayle, who shrank away against the wall.

Getting hold of her, he jerked her up and dragged her across the room towards the fire.

Miss Frayle struggled frantically, inarticulate sounds issuing from her gag.

With a snarl of rage, Lorrimer suddenly extended his hands around her throat and started to strangle her.

Then the door of the shed was kicked open from the outside, and Dr. Morelle, followed by the Inspector and Jackson, came rushing in.

Peter Lorrimer dropped his hands from Miss Frayle's throat and dived for the door.

Expertly the two police officers caught hold of him, and after a short sharp struggle, brought him under control.

Meanwhile Dr. Morelle was attending to Miss Frayle.

Quickly he untied her hands and removed the handkerchief gag. Miss Frayle lay limply against him with her eyes closed. Very tenderly, he looked at the imprints of Lorrimer's fingers on her neck. Very gently, he began to massage her throat.

"That's very nice!" Miss Frayle murmured, her eyes still closed.

"Miss Frayle!"

At Dr. Morelle's sharp exclamation, Miss Frayle opened her eyes and smiled lovingly at him.

"I knew you'd get here in time!"

Dr. Morelle gave her a severe look. "May I point out that if only you'd obeyed my instructions, it wouldn't have been necessary to come here at all!"

He helped her to her feet, where she swayed unsteadily in his arms.

Nearby, Peter Lorrimer was being firmly held by Inspector Harris and Jackson. He was staring straight in front of him with glazed and staring eyes. Suddenly he shivered violently, blinked his eyes rapidly, and looked around him with a puzzled, vacant expression.

"Where am I?" he muttered. "What's happening?" He stared at his captors. "Who are you?"

After making sure that Miss Frayle was sufficiently recovered to stand on her feet, Dr. Morelle crossed over to Peter Lorrimer.

"You don't remember me, Mr. Lorrimer?"

"No." Lorrimer appeared bewildered, then: "Yes! You're Captain Welton."

Dr. Morelle smiled faintly. "No longer, I'm afraid. I have abandoned the publishing business in favour of detection."

"Detecting what?"

"A murderer, Mr. Lorrimer."

Lorrimer looked at him in confusion. "But, I don't understand."

"You soon will," Dr. Morelle said implacably. He turned to Inspector Harris. "And now I suggest we return to Barren Tor, so that we can settle matters with Mr. Kimber as well."

* * * * * * *

In his study, Kimber was still lying back in his wheelchair, staring ahead with fixed, unblinking eyes. Dr. Morelle was seated at the desk opposite him as before, but now Miss Frayle, with Peter Lorrimer between the Inspector and Jackson, were

seated round in a rough semi-circle.

"And now," Dr. Morelle resumed, "I think we can deal with the final phase of this somewhat unusual case." He leaned forward, and passed his fingers two or three times across Kimber's eyes. He spoke in a low voice:

"Mr. Kimber. This is Dr. Morelle speaking. Wake up, Mr. Kimber!"

Kimber shivered violently, blinking his eyes rapidly several times. Suddenly he sat up and looked around him with a bewildered expression, which rapidly turned into one of anger.

"What's happening here?" he demanded." His puzzled gaze settled on the two policemen, before swinging back to Dr. Morelle. "Who are these two men?"

"These are Inspector Harris and Detective-Sergeant Jackson of the County Police."

Kimber visibly flinched. "Police!"

"Mr. Lorrimer you know," Dr. Morelle resumed. "Also Amy...."

As Kimber took in the presence of Peter Lorrimer and Miss Frayle, he betrayed a quick flash of alarm.

"...alias my personal assistant, Miss Frayle."

Apparently realizing that he was in a tight corner, Kimber tried to bluster.

"Get out of my house, all of you! Get out this moment!"

"You're being a little hasty, Mr. Kimber," Dr. Morelle said. "These gentlemen are anxious to have a few words with you."

"I've got nothing to say to them," Kimber snapped.

Dr. Morelle smiled grimly. "Perhaps you will have, when I tell you that you have already given them the full details of your dastardly plot."

"I've given them details?" Kimber was clearly shaken. "Of my plot?"

"Certainly—while in an hypnotic trance which I induced," Dr. Morelle said smugly. "Rather a case of the biter bit, isn't it, Mr. Kimber?"

Kimber was now thoroughly frightened. "You hypnotized

me?"

Dr. Morelle nodded grimly. "What you said in the trance may not be filed in evidence against you. But Miss Frayle here is a material witness. She will identify the charred bones in the incinerator as those of your stepdaughter by means of this earring...." He paused as he picked up a sapphire earring from the desk, holding it before him..."which was found by her a moment or two before Bensall was murdered. So if you will take my advice, Mr. Kimber, you will do well to make a free and frank confession of how you plotted to get rid of your stepdaughter by hypnotising Peter Lorrimer, and using him to murder for you by proxy."

Before Kimber could make any response to the damning accusation, Peter Lorrimer leapt to his feet. His face blazing with anger, he rushed at Kimber, and caught him by the throat.

He began shaking Kimber to and fro like a dog with a rat.

"You swine! You devil! You made me kill her—and I never knew! You made me kill Cynthia, whom I loved, whom I was going to marry. You devil, I'll kill you for it!"

Recovering from their surprise, the Inspector and Jackson jumped forward. Getting hold of Peter Lorrimer, they managed to drag him away from Kimber, who was now cowering in his chair, all resistance gone.

"So you see," Dr. Morelle resumed, "what was coming to you, Mr. Kimber—if your plot had succeeded."

The others looked their puzzlement.

"But it did succeed!" Inspector Harris exclaimed.

Dr. Morelle shook his head, smiling thinly: "On the contrary. You see, he *thought* he had hypnotized this young man, but in actual fact he *hadn't*!"

"What are you talking about?" Lorrimer demanded.

"Peter Lorrimer," Dr. Morelle explained complacently, "is resistant to any hypnotic influence. I tested him myself when I called on him in my capacity of Captain Welton. But when Mr. Kimber decided to test his amateur capabilities on him, with commendable initiative Peter Lorrimer seized on this golden

opportunity."

Miss Frayle showed a sudden flash of insight. "You mean, he only *pretended* to be hypnotized, but wasn't?"

"Precisely, my dear Miss Frayle. And quite apart from his natural immunity to hypnotism, had Mr. Lorrimer really loved Cynthia, it is very doubtful that he could have been hypnotized to kill her. Kimber, as an amateur, probably wasn't aware of that."

Peter Lorrimer's eyes blazed with anger. "You must be mad! Why in heaven's name should I want to kill the girl I was going to marry!"

"Because...." Dr. Morelle picked up some notes, which were lying before him on the desk, "...because, firstly, you knew it would be a bigamous marriage, seeing that you were married in Birmingham on the 14th of April last to a Miss Lucy Adams, who is alive today."

Lorrimer remained silent, staring at Dr. Morelle with baleful intensity.

"And secondly," Dr. Morelle resumed, "because in the desk in your cottage lies Cynthia Mason's will, leaving everything to you."

Dr. Morelle paused, and looked at Miss Frayle, smiling sardonically. "I heard all about Cynthia's *mother's* will from Miss Frayle...who, with her well-known capacity for searching for haystacks in needles, naturally missed the one document which elucidated the whole matter."

Miss Frayle blushed and squirmed in her seat, both indignant and ashamed of hearing her efforts thus described.

Following Dr. Morelle's revelations, everyone in the room was looking at Peter Lorrimer, except Kimber, who was hunched up in his chair with his face in his hands.

"Cynthia Mason was murdered deliberately and cold-bloodedly by Peter Lorrimer," Dr. Morelle went on implacably. "He did not, however, kill Bensall. That was Mr. Kimber's work"

Kimber looked up at this. "It's not true—I deny it!" she said shrilly. "How could I? I'm a cripple—I can't get down to the

incinerator shed."

Inspector Harris, who had been following the revelations with a furrowed brow, shot a glance at Dr. Morelle. "Doctor—?"

"Kindly note the first piece of evidence, Inspector. Mr. Kimber knew that Bensall had been killed in the incinerator shed. A fact known only to Miss Frayle, you, me, and the murderer."

"It's nonsense," Kimber protested, "all this—lying nonsense...."

"Now for the second piece of evidence," Dr. Morelle said complacently. He reached into a drawer of Kimber's desk, and extracted from it a bloodstained handkerchief.

"Miss Frayle's handkerchief, with which she tried to staunch Bensall's wound, and which you found when you went to recover the body. I saw it in your drawer on the occasion when you so kindly went to assist Miss Frayle with the kitchen boiler."

"It's preposterous, what you're saying." Kimber remained defiant. "The handkerchief is mine—I cut my hand...."

Dr. Morelle's voice cut like a lash. "It is now you who is talking nonsense, Mr. Kimber. A third piece of evidence—a rather sensational piece...."

He took from his pocket a small photograph, which he held up with its reverse side to Kimber.

"...a photograph of *you*, Mr. Kimber, in the act of murdering Bensall!"

With a strangled cry, Kimber jumped to his feet from the wheelchair and ran to Dr. Morelle to snatch the photograph from him.

Dr. Morelle calmly turned the face of the photograph so that Kimber could now see it for what it really was—a snapshot of a small child.

Kimber immediately halted, suddenly realizing that he had given away the fact that he could walk.

"A rather dubious little ruse, but it appears to have worked," Dr. Morelle commented dryly, returning the photograph to his pocket. "The photograph is, in point of fact, of a small niece of

mine—but my little deception has established that Mr. Kimber's footwork is as nimble as yours and mine.

"The purpose of his pretence to be crippled was, of course, in the first place, to play on his stepdaughter's sympathies, so that she would be less likely to contemplate leaving him."

Kimber, realizing that the game was up, sank back again into his wheelchair.

"I think, Inspector," Dr. Morelle said, "there is little doubt that we now have sufficient evidence to take Mr. Kimber and Mr. Lorrimer to the gallows."

Their attention lately having been given entirely to Kimber and Dr. Morelle, both the Inspector and Jackson had unwittingly relaxed their grip on Peter Lorrimer.

Suddenly he threw off their detaining hands and rushed for the door and out into the hall.

Inspector Harris reacted belatedly. "After him! Quick!"

He rushed out after Lorrimer, followed by Dr. Morelle and Miss Frayle. Jackson stayed behind to guard the scowling Kimber.

Peter Lorrimer was making for the front door when he saw a uniformed policeman standing before it, fully alert and ready to block his exit.

Instead he veered off and rushed up the stairs, to be hotly pursued by Inspector Harris and the policeman.

Dr. Morelle, however, continued to make straight for the front door, dutifully followed by Miss Frayle.

Outside the house a light now came on in an upstairs window. The window was then thrown open, and a body appeared to dive out of it headfirst into the night.

There was a dull, crunching thud as Lorrimer's body hit the drive, the actual impact invisible in the darkness.

Dr. Morelle hurried forward, and far above him. Inspector Harris became silhouetted in the window.

Sick with horror, Miss Frayle turned away, leaning against the front door frame, breathing hard.

She turned as Dr. Morelle moved back to her. "Is he...?" She

was unable to complete her whispered sentence.

"Killed instantaneously," Dr. Morelle said gently. "Perhaps it's the best way out."

As Miss Frayle began shivering violently, Dr. Morelle put his arn round her shoulders. She turned to him and gazed into his face....

* * * * * * *

In Dr. Morelle's Harley Street study, Dr. Morelle was still dictating his account of the affair of the missing heiress, and Miss Frayle was busily taking it down in shorthand.

"And as I gazed deep into Miss Frayle's strained white face...."

Miss Frayle's pencil stopped. She gazed lovingly at Dr Morelle, a tremulous smile upon her lips.

"...I breathed a silent prayer of gratitude to my creator that he had endowed me with sufficient commonsense to remain a bachelor."

Dr. Morelle leaned back and gazed blandly at the ceiling, blowing smoke rings.

Miss Frayle's tremulous smile changed to an expression of disgruntled disappointment—and there came the sound of a sharp click as she jabbed viciously at her notebook—and again broke the point of her pencil.

THE CASE OF
THE QUEENPIN

Doctor Morelle has visited the majority of the countries of the globe. He has lectured in New York and Paris, Capetown and Ottawa, Belgrade and Auckland. But in recent years he has rarely moved from London. He says that, in spite of all the losses resulting from the war, the library facilities of London—as necessary for the abstruse researches in which he is so often concerned—are as good as anywhere in the world. And his house in Harley Street has for him become more of a home than any other residence which he has occupied in the past twenty years or so.

As a result he usually shows a marked reluctance to leave London for medical purposes, and he has been known to turn down an offer to undertake a consultation in some distant city, even when the fee offered is considerable, merely because he does not wish to spend any length of time away from Britain's capital.

It was, however, both the offer of a tempting fee, and the fact that the offer came from an old friend and colleague whom he did not like to 'let down', that made him travel to the old city of Kingston-upon-Hull (commonly known as Hull) in order to take part in a joint consultation concerning a young man afflicted with the distressing mental condition known as paranoia.

The case did not prove as complex as he had feared, and Doctor Morelle and his medical friend, now installed in a comfortable practice in Hull, were soon able to come to an

agreement as to the best course of treatment to be pursued. When this stage had been reached, Doctor Morelle returned to the pleasant hotel where he had taken the precaution of booking rooms. In the lounge he found Miss Frayle waiting for him. It was fairly late in the evening, and she seemed to be more than a trifle anxious, though the Doctor was unable to see the reason for her anxiety.

"Oh, there you are, Doctor Morelle," she said in somewhat relieved tones as he entered the hotel lounge. "I was just beginning to wonder whatever had happened to you."

"Psychological consultations are frequently of considerable duration. Miss Frayle," he replied in an irritated manner, and then relaxing a little, he went on: "I trust, however, that you have been able to occupy your evening in a profitable manner."

Miss Frayle smiled. "Oh, yes, Doctor," she said. "I've been to the pictures. It was a lovely film, all about the life of a young doctor. He was so attractive and charming." She paused and sighed deeply. "The film was nothing at all like real life, of course."

Doctor Morelle found a certain source of irritation in Miss Frayle's romantic outlook on life, and the present was, he thought, one of the most unpleasing of such occasions.

"I regret," he said, "that members of the medical profession in some strange manner known only to themselves fail to conform to your sentimental imaginings."

Miss Frayle sighed again. "Oh, well," she said, "I suppose that you can't have everything in this life."

She looked around her carefully, as if she wanted to be sure that no one was sufficiently near to overhear what she was saying. Indeed, the only other occupant of the lounge—an elderly gentleman with a red face—was clearly buried in his copy of *The Times*, which he was reading with such care and attention that it was clear enough that he would not be bothered to listen to any conversation which might be taking place. And he now left them.

Miss Frayle grasped the Doctor's arm convulsively. "Doctor,"

she murmured in dramatic tones, "there's something queer going on in this hotel."

The Doctor looked even more irritated than was his wont. Lack of precision on the part of anyone to whom he was talking was always one of the things which most annoyed him.

"What precisely does that exceedingly vague remark imply, Miss Frayle?" he demanded.

Miss Fravle looked somewhat taken aback by this demand to make any sort of precise formulation of what it was that had struck her as being queer about the hotel, but she knew that she would have to give the Doctor some justification for what she had said.

"Well, while I've been waiting here for you," she remarked, "people have been bustling in and out, and the Manager looks simply worried to death. Then—I'm sure that there's something very peculiar going on—a man popped into this lounge just now, and, before he went out again in a hurry—he gave me the strangest look."

Doctor Morelle looked completely nonplussed by this recital of what Miss Fayle regarded as the facts of the case.

"You amaze me, Miss Frayle!" he exclaimed. "Ah, I am afraid that your ever-fervid imagination has been somewhat overstimulated by the cinematic exhibition which you have been witnessing during my absence in the hospital."

Miss Frayle was not convinced by this apparently reasonable explanation of the matters that had been exciting her during the Doctor's absence.

"But, Doctor, I tell you," she began to expostulate, and then broke off. "Look!" she exclaimed, "there's the man now—the man I was talking about. He's just coming in again. And the Manager is with him."

"Good evening, Doctor Morelle," said the newcomer, holding out his hand and smiling in a friendly manner. "I'm Detective-Inspector Grant. I thought that I recognized your Miss Frayle when I was in here earlier on."

Miss Frayle giggled helplessly. "Oh, is that why you stared so

hard at me," she said.

The Inspector laughed. "Yes, that's right, Miss Frayle," he said. "Sorry if it worried you. But that's what becomes of being famous, you see."

Doctor Morelle frowned portentously, and the Inspector caught a glimpse of his expression, adding quickly: "And, of course, being assistant to someone famous too."

Doctor Morelle seemed to be getting impatient at the course of this conversation.

"I presume," he said, "that your object in honouring us with this unexpected visit is not entirely due to your desire to pay us compliments."

The Inspector appeared a little surprised at this sudden wordy onslaught.

"Indeed, no, Doctor," he said hastily, "though, naturally, it's pleasant to meet people so well known as Miss Frayle and yourself. But the moment the Manager here told me that you were staying in his hotel, I knew that you were the one man who would be able to help me in the little job which is on my plate tonight."

"I knew that something queer was going on here," announced Miss Frayle in tones of triumph, utter and unconcealed. "What exactly has been happening?"

"It's nothing much, really," the Manager hastily explained. "But if it gets at all generally known in the neighbourhood, it's sure that it won't do my hotel any good."

Inspector Grant grinned. "Nonsense!" he said. "Whatever happens, nobody's going to blame *you* for it. What's happened is in no way your fault, after all."

"I'm not so sure," the Manager replied. "You know how people talk in a place like this."

Doctor Morelle was getting more and more impatient and annoyed at the way in which things were developing.

"Perhaps," he said, "Inspector Grant would be so kind as to divulge to me the cause of your apprehension. After all, your cryptic utterances are completely meaningless to me, and I

should like to be enlightened a little—that is. Inspector, if the whole affair is not of too confidential a nature to be divulged to anyone outside the immediate circle of those concerned."

The Inspector at once became very apologetic,

"I'm very sorry, Doctor, to have rattled on like that without giving you any explanation," he said. "As a matter of fact, I was just going to tell you all about it. Between you and me—and Miss Frayle, of course!—we've run a notorious fence to earth. She's been staying in this hotel. Name of Carla Donetti. She is, in effect, the kingpin of an organised bunch of crooks who we've been after for a long time."

Miss Frayle giggled impulsively. "Surely you mean the *queen*pin, Inspector," she corrected him,

"That's right, Miss," he said with a laugh. "As a matter of fact, they've been blowing round the country knocking off a lot of very valuable pictures—old masters and all that. They've been cutting them out of the frames, and then disposing of them to unscrupulous collectors on the continent."

The Manager added seriously: "To look at her," he said, "she is the last sort of person that you'd expect to be engaged in that sort of business, you know. Always dressed in the absolute height of fashion—smart, elegant...."

"On the contrary," Doctor Morelle interrupted him, "your description at once suggests to me the type of individual who might well be expected to be engaging herself in nefarious practices of all kinds."

"The Doctor," Miss Frayle patiently explained, "does not altogether approve of smart, elegant women, Mr. Denham."

Doctor Morelle cast a meaningful glance at Miss Frayle. "No doubt our friend the Manager will have observed that for himself," he retorted.

While Miss Frayle was endeavouring to extract the meaning of this venomous thrust, the Doctor was resuming his conversation with Inspector Grant,

"You were saying, Inspector," he went on to ask, "that you have trapped the woman at this hotel?"

The Inspector rubbed his nose ruefully with the back of his hand.

"That's just what we haven't done, I'm afraid, Doctor," he said. "She's managed to give us the slip, just when we were ready to close the net and get hold of the whole gang of crooks. Most unfortunate bit of timing."

"Oh, dear!" Miss Frayle murmured, feeling entirely sympathetic with the Inspector in his plight.

The Inspector, however, resumed a little more cheerfully: "But I've picked up her maid, who had also been staying here. Of course, it doesn't necessarily follow that she's in any way implicated in the crimes, but I'm just going to ask her a few questions. I'd be very glad if you'd stay here and give me any helpful tips as to what she has to say, Doctor."

Mr. Denham, the Manager, now said: "Here's your Sergeant now, Inspector, with the girl."

"Oh, yes." Inspector Grant replied. "Thank you, Sergeant. Come and sit down, Miss," he added to the girl who was glancing around her in an alarmed fashion. "There's no need to be frightened. All I want is to know what you know of a Miss Donetti. Oh, Mr. Denham," he said, turning to the Manager.

"Yes, Inspector?"

"There's no need for us to detain you here any longer. I'm sure that you're a very busy man, and won't have a lot of time to spare over this business. I'll keep you well posted as to what happens from now on."

"Thanks," said the Manager, seeing that this amounted to his dismissal from the scene.

"Now," said the Inspector, when the Manager had left the room, "let's have your name again."

"My name's Molly O'Brien," the girl said, with a very definite trace of Irish brogue in her speech. "And I'm only over here from Ireland this six months."

Doctor Morelle looked interested. "What part of Ireland do you come from?" he asked.

Molly O'Brien looked gently surprised at this question. She

was an attractive girl with dark curly hair, and her early fright-ened expression now seemed to have left her face. Clearly she realized that the best that she could do was to tell the truth.

"I come from Ballymoney, in the North of Ireland, sir," she said. "I got my job with Miss Donetti from an employ-ment agency in Liverpool, and since then—during the past six months, as I said—I've been travelling about with her all over the country."

"What sort of places did you go to with Miss Donetti, Molly?" asked the Inspector.

"Oh, all over the place," she explained. "Plymouth, Bristol, Swansea, Cardiff, Portsmouth...."

"And you enjoyed your job?" the Inspector asked.

Molly smiled. And her smile was a pleasant sight to see.

"Sure," she said, "Miss Donetti is a grand person. We have always stayed at the best hotels, wherever we went. Mind you, I don't know the first thing about her business. She hardly encour-aged me to ask any questions about her personal affairs, and so I didn't."

"I see," said the Inspector. This, as he had said to Doctor Morelle a few minutes earlier, was just what he had expected. "And now let's get round to this afternoon. Tell me just what happened, will you? She went out directly after tea, and, as you know, she hasn't come back yet."

"She did so," said Molly, with the emphasis on the last word of the sentence.

Miss Frayle's forehead puckered up in surprise, and bewil-derment at this response on Molly's part.

"You mean she did go out, but didn't come back?" Miss Frayle asked.

"She did so," Molly repeated.

The Inspector grinned cheerfully. "I think I know what she means all right, Miss Frayle," he said. "Now, Molly, when she went out, did she take anything with her?"

"I packed a small suitcase for her," Molly said, "and that's about all. She gave me a fair amount of money, and said that

maybe I'd not be seeing her again for about two weeks. I was to stay on here, she told me, until I heard from her, But that wouldn't be for some time."

The Inspector looked a little perturbed at this information. It was more or less what he had anticipated, but it was annoying to think that his quarry had escaped him with such a small margin of time and yet so completely.

Doctor Morelle apparently was in no way worried at what had happened, though he clearly considered that there was no more information to obtained from Molly.

"Did she receive any visitors at these various hotels where she stayed?" he asked.

"She did," Molly said with a smile, which suggested infinite possibilities. "Sometimes two or three of them in one place. They were nearly all men. I often thought to meself that Miss Donetti was a bit of a flighty one."

Doctor Morelle looked annoyed and irritated. "I'm not asking you for your impressions," he snapped. "Kindly keep to the facts that you know for certain."

Molly looked a trifle sulky at this rebuke. "Sure," she said, "a girl has a right to her own thoughts without having her head bitten off when she...."

Doctor Morelle interrupted her ruthlessly. "Were there any visitors coming to see her during her stay at *this* hotel?" he asked with considerable emphasis.

"There were not," Molly replied, her lips still pursed up sulkily. "Faith, we'd only been here two days, so we had, and I suppose that Miss Donetti had scarcely had time to get to know any of the folk here."

The door of the lounge swung open suddenly, and the Manager rushed in, his face contorted with excitement.

"Inspector! Doctor Morelle!" he exclaimed in tones that were almost triumphant with delight and excitement.

"What's biting you now, Mr. Denham?" asked Inspector Grant. The Inspector, in. fact, was more than a little annoyed at this interruption, for he had thought that the cross-examination

of Molly O'Brien was just showing signs of yielding results of some promise.

"A man has just called at the hotel," Mr. Denham explained.

"And what about it?"

"He's asked for Miss Donetti," the Manager said, still very excited in manner.

"Where is he?" exclaimed the Inspector, realizing the vast importance of this news. "You didn't let him go, did you? You managed to keep him here somehow? This may be the very thing to lead us to Donetti."

The Manager smiled, with confidence in his own common-sense and good judgment.

"No, I didn't let him go," he said. "I asked him if he would mind waiting a few minutes. And then your Sergeant told him that he knew you would like a word with him."

Inspector Grant looked relieved at this news. "That's good," he said, rubbing his hands together in a satisfied manner. "Bring him in here right away, will you, Mr. Denham?"

As he went to the door the Manager explained. "He says his name is Bennett. I'll get him and send him into you, Inspector, right away."

Miss Frayle looked duly impressed by the way in which Inspector Grant was handling the case. "You think that he may be able to tell us something about Miss Donetti, and what has happened to her, Inspector?" she asked,

"Maybe," the Inspector said. "That is, of course, if he will tell us what he knows. But then, perhaps you'll be able to persuade him to tell us a thing or two, Doctor,"

Doctor Morelle smiled sardonically. "That," he said, "depends in essence upon whether or no he has anything to conceal. After all, we must bear in mind that as yet we have no information whatsoever on that not unimportant point."

Bennett, when he came in, proved to be a middle-aged man of quite ordinary appearance, dressed in a dark lounge suit and carrying a raincoat over one arm. He looked a little surprised at what was happening.

"What's all this about, gentleman?" he remarked as he entered. "I came along here to call on Miss Donetti, and I seem somehow to have got myself mixed up with some police matter. Can you tell me what is happening?"

Inspector Grant knew how to deal with this sort of approach.

"Sorry to trouble you. Mr. Bennett," he said in soothing tones, "but it so happens that we are rather interested in the lady whose name you mentioned. As she isn't here to speak for herself, we wondered if perhaps you might have some information about her, which would enable us to fill in the gaps in our knowledge. This, incidentally, is Miss Frayle, and this is Doctor Morelle."

Bennett looked at Doctor Morelle, His jaw dropped, as if he had been very surprised. Then he smiled at Miss Frayle. She giggled and nodded. There seemed to be a sense of embarrassment and tenseness in the air.

"This," Inspector Grant went on, "is Molly O'Brien. She is Miss Donetti's maid, and she has been able to give us a certain amount of information about her employer."

"Good evening, sir," Molly said, with a smile which mixed demureness and pertness.

The Inspector was studying Bennett's face with some care as he made these introductions. It seemed that the detective thought that it was possible that the man in some way might give himself away when faced by the others. But such was not the case. Bennett did not give any sign of perturbation.

"Possibly, though," Inspector Grant said, "you have already met Miss O'Brien during your period of friendship, or acquaintanceship, with Miss Donetti?"

Bennett shook his head decisively. "I'm afraid not." he pointed out. "As a matter of fact, you see, I've never even met Miss Donetti myself yet."

This was quite clearly a considerable surprise to Inspector Grant, and possibly he was a trifle disappointed also. This, however, he did not reveal in an open way.

He merely raised his eyebrows slightly and glanced at Doctor

Morelle.

The Doctor said, in rasping tones: "Indeed? Then I am afraid, Mr. Bennett, that the doubtful pleasure of meeting her is something of which you will have to face the postponement. I trust that it will not cause you too much pain."

The Inspector smiled gently at this sally, and resumed his cross-examination with the question: "What exactly were you wanting to see Miss Donetti about tonight, Mr. Bennett?"

Bennett hesitated before replying. It appeared as if he was conscious that here he was skating upon thin ice, and was very doubtful of just what reply would be both truthful and tactful. He coughed and shuffled his feet.

Then he said; "Well, I suppose there's no reason why you shouldn't have the truth about the business. The fact of the matter is that I deal in jewellery—valuable stuff, you know—in a small way. I'm an amateur, and make quite a hobby out of buying and selling small pieces. Miss Donetti sent me a message that she had some jewellery she wanted to dispose of. She asked me if I would call here tonight, about this time, when she hoped to be able to show me some stuff, which she thought would interest me. That was all it amounted to, and that is why I was so surprised when I found that she wasn't available."

Doctor Morelle listened to this description with a smile of withering scepticism on his lips. He was obviously not in any way impressed by what Bennett had told them.

"How did Miss Donetti come to hear of you and your amateur efforts at dealing in jewellery, Mr. Bennett?" he asked, and there was more than a hint of sarcasm in his tone which did not escape Bennett's attention.

Bennett waved his hand airily. "I'm quite well known around here," he said.

"Indeed?" queried Doctor Morelle. "You are a resident in Hull of some long standing, then?"

"Oh, yes," Bennett replied suavely. "I've lived here for some ten years or so."

"But your deals are purely private affairs, aren't they?" asked

the Inspector.

"Yes, quite private. But these things get known. You can't keep them altogether to yourself. And anybody who wants to do a deal soon gets to hear if me, you know."

Doctor Morelle still looked sceptical.

"And you wish to imply that this is how Miss Donetti got to know of you, no doubt?" he asked.

Bennett grinned. "Well, as I have already said, I'd never met her, and I assumed that she had been put on to me by some mutual friend who knew about my deals in jewellery, and thought that Miss Donetti and I might find each other useful. That is the explanation that I can give you, and I don't know of any other. If you have any different suggestion to make, I shall be pleased to say if I think it at all likely."

The inspector stroked his chin thoughtfully. This, it appeared, was not the kind of explanation that he had anticipated, but he realized that it was a moderately convincing story, and one that would not be at all easy to disprove. Leaving Bennett for a moment, he turned to Molly O'Brien.

"Did you know that this gentleman would be calling to see Miss Donetti tonight?" he asked the maid,

"I'd no notion of it," she replied. "Miss Donetti said nothing to me about anyone calling. But then she didn't tell me anything about her private affairs. as I told you just now."

"Were you aware," Doctor Morelle interjected, "that your employer had in her possession some jewellery, which she was desirous of selling to Mr. Bennett or to anyone else?"

"She never told me," Molly persisted stubbornly. "I know nothing at all about her business or her private affairs."

The Inspector had now made up his mind. It was clear to him that the moment for action had cone. And Inspector Grant was a man of action who did not hesitate to move when it was clear to him that the circumstances demanded movement.

"Mr. Bennett," he said thoughtfully, "I wonder if you'd mind popping along to the station with me so that I could check up on one or two points, and get a statement written out, which you

could then sign? You see, we are very anxious to get in touch with Miss Donetti, and you are possibly the only person available at the moment, who can assist us in our search for her."

Bennett looked slightly alarmed. "Surely," he said, "that isn't altogether necessary, Inspector. I've told you all I know. As I have said, I never met Miss Donetti, and I think it's very unlikely that anything I can do will help you to find her. Besides, my wife is waiting for me at home. It's getting late, and she'll be very anxious if I keep her waiting very much longer. You know what the ladies are like,"

"Yes, indeed," said Miss Frayle in her usual sympathetic way.

"Is your wife on the phone?" the Inspector asked quietly.

"Yes," Bennett replied,

The Inspector smiled. "That's all right, then," he said. "You can just ring her up and let her know that you are having a chat with the police. Explain that it's nothing serious, and that you expect to be home in an hour or two."

"It's all a bit of a nuisance," Bennett grumbled. "Still, if you insist, Inspector."

He fumbled in his pocket, fished out a handful of money, and said: "Is there a call-box anywhere about, do you know?"

"Yes," answered Miss Frayle. "There is one just by the reception desk. It's one of those slot things, you know."

"Have I got any coppers?" Bennett murmured. "Only one penny, I'm afraid. Can anyone lend me another penny, please?"

Miss Frayle opened her handbag, looked in it for a moment, produced a coin, and handed it over.

"There you are, Mr. Bennett," she said with a smile.

"Thanks very much." Bennett replied, smiling in his turn. "I'll pay you back, you know." He made his way to the door, saying as he went, "I won't be a minute, then, Inspector. It's only a local call, so it will only take a moment to put through. Then I'll be right back again."

Doctor Morelle had been watching the proceedings carefully for the last few minutes. Now he held up his hand in a minatory gesture,

"I think that you'd better stay right where you are, Mr. Bennett!" he exclaimed. "Before you go out to telephone you have a considerable amount of explaining to do."

"What do you mean?" Bennett expostulated.

"Yes, what's the idea, Doctor?" asked Inspector Grant in considerable surprise.

"Merely that I suspect this man knows a good deal more about this Donetti person than he has so far admitted," said Doctor Morelle slowly. "I think that you should ask him some more questions before you allow him to leave our presence."

Miss Frayle put her hand to her mouth. "Look out, Inspector!" she screamed.

Indeed, Bennett was making for the door as fast as he could go.

"No you don't!" Inspector Grant exclaimed, hurling himself rapidly across the room. "You stay put, my man! I want to know a good deal more about you than you've yet told me."

He grabbed the man by the arm, and Bennett wriggled madly in the attempt to get rid of the detective's grip. But Inspector Grant had graduated in a hard school—the school of dockland—and he was used to almost every kind of rough house,

"Blast you!" grunted Bennett. "Keep your hands off me."

"I shouldn't struggle if I were you," the Inspector said. "You might get hurt. You come along quietly to the station, and everything will be all right. Otherwise I don't know what might happen."

"If you will kindly remain here, Miss Frayle," Doctor Morelle said, "I will accompany Inspector Grant and his guest to the Police Station. I do not anticipate that I shall be absent for more than half an hour or so, and when I return I shall doubtless be able to satisfy what inordinate curiosity as to the course of events in Hull which is no doubt, at this precise moment, so agitating your restless mind."

The next half hour seemed a long time to Miss Frayle. She sat down and tried to read, but she found her attention wandering from the book. Then she walked up and down the lounge, but

found that all the time one insistent question was hammering in her mind. If it was true that Bennett was an accomplice of Miss Donetti—and his behaviour seemed to place that beyond all doubt—how had Doctor Morelle realized the fact? The doctor always said that every criminal made a mistake, and the alert mind should be able to spot that mistake. Miss Frayle could only conclude that her mind was not efficiently alert for the purpose.

At length, however, the Doctor returned. He looked more than ordinarily pleased with himself, and as he came in he was rubbing his hands together in a satisfied manner,

"I think that we have performed a very satisfactory evening's work, my dear Miss Frayle," he said.

"Why, what happened at the Police Station?" she asked

"Under interrogation by the estimable Inspector Grant, Bennett revealed that he was indeed an accomplice of the Donettt woman. He has divulged an address in the South of England where she can be found, and I have no doubt that within a matter of hours at most both she and sundry other confederates will be duly. apprehended and incarcerated under lock and key."

"It's an astonishing piece of work Doctor!" Miss Frayle said.

"Moderately simple, though," the Doctor added in self-satisfied tones.

"I must say," added Miss Frayle, "that it was pretty smart of you to catch on to the fact that he really had no intention of phoning his wife, but was merely using the phone call as an excuse to make a getaway."

"His request for the loan of a second penny is what made me quite certain of his complicity in the crime," Doctor Morelle explained patiently.

"I don't see why," Miss Frayle objected. "After all, everyone knows that you have to put twopence in a public telephone in order to make a local call."

"On the contrary," Doctor Morelle corrected her, "that request for a second penny proved the complete falsity of his earlier claim that he was an old resident of Hull—of, if I remember

aright, ten years standing."

Miss Frayle was puzzled. "But why, Doctor?" she asked in a bewildered way. "What did it prove?"

"It proved that he could have been in Hull for only a comparatively short time," the Doctor said.

"Why?"

"The charge for a local call from a public telephone booth in this city, my dear Miss Frayle, is one penny only."

Miss Frayle looked more surprised than ever. "Is that really so, Doctor?" she asked.

"Indubitably," the Doctor replied.

"How you find out these thing is what amazes me!" Miss Frayle exclaimed.

"The fact has been fairly widely publicised of late in the columns of the national Press," Doctor Morelle said in complacent tones. "Those who do not confine themselves to the more sensational headlines and the advertisements of the more erotic types of films would have noted the report."

"You wouldn't be taking a dig at me, would you?" asked Miss Frayle with a giggle. The Doctor ignored this remark.

"It is true," he went on, "that my superior acumen enabled me to discern the fatal error which was made by Bennett under cross-examination. The error would doubtless have escaped notice had I been a person of merely average intelligence."

Miss Frayle smiled. "There is one other question I have been meaning to ask you ever since we came to Hull, Doctor Morelle," she said.

"Yes, my dear Miss Frayle," he answered, now quite complacent, since the case had been brought to such a satisfactory conclusion. "What further information would you wish me to vouchsafe you?"

"You remember," she said, "that you came down here to advise on a case of paranoia."

"Precisely."

"What exactly does the word paranoia mean? I've been wondering ever since we arrived."

Doctor Morelle snorted impatiently, "It is a perfectly ordinary word, in general use in the medical profession, Miss Frayle," he replied, "It means chronic delusive obsession with one's own self-importance."

Miss Frayle giggled. "Ah!" she exclaimed. "I thought it was something of the sort. That explains it."

"Explains what, may I ask?" snarled the Doctor.

"Why they called *you* into consultation," murmured Miss Frayle.

THE CASE OF THE
MAN IN THE CAR

Freda Hopkins had never liked her name. As soon as she left her secondary school, she contrived to add a letter to her Christian name. 'Frieda' was much more distinctive, redolent of some foreign origin, suggestive perhaps of a château on the Danube or a cabaret in Budapest. She clung tenaciously to 'Frieda', and her ever-growing circle of male admirers was duly impressed. It seemed to fit in with her tawny hair, grey-green eyes, and slightly mysterious air.

Since her father's death, Frieda had travelled around quite a lot with her mother, who had a fair-sized private income. They favoured resorts such as Bournemouth, Southport, Leamington, and Buxton, where there was a certain amount of congenial company for Mrs. Hopkins, and a fair supply of eligible males for Frieda. For nearly four years, she danced, played tennis, flirted, and generally frittered away time to her heart's content. But she still disliked her second name. True, one or two of her more serious admirers had suggested that she might care to change it, but on careful inquiry from Mrs. Hopkins they had proved singularly lacking in this world's goods; indeed, two of them were under the distinct impression that Frieda had a substantial income which could be accommodated to the needs of a penniless husband. In fact, none of her various young male friends seemed to be overblessed with riches, and Frieda had to have money.

"My daughter is accustomed to a certain standard of living,"

Mrs. Hopkins would inform would-be suitors in a dignified tone that was always sufficient to deter the most ardent of them. It was not until Mrs. Hopkins took a small furnished flat at Worthing, and began to entertain Frieda's friends in a slightly more domesticated style, that she began to attract the rather more dependable type of man.

Among them was Malcolm Sutcliffe, a prosperous chartered accountant from Sevenoaks, where he had inherited a thriving business from his uncle. He was ten years older than Frieda, but Mrs. Hopkins dismissed this as the merest bagatelle, and threw them into each other's company as frequently as possible. After Malcolm's week's holiday was over, he continued to motor down to Worthing quite frequently at weekends, and on Frieda's twenty-first birthday, their engagement was announced.

Mrs. Hopkins' death following a seizure hastened their marriage, and within the year, Frieda found herself mistress of a charming imitation Tudor residence, standing in three acres of grounds in the little village of Dockham, five miles from Sevenoaks, in the midst of a wooded hillside.

For the first few months, the novelty of her new life absorbed her completely. Malcolm had a fairly wide circle of friends, who were quite interesting at first acquaintance, but whom she later came to regard as dull in the extreme. Frieda had not much affinity with the businessman type or his wife. She began to wonder why she had married Malcolm, regretting that she had not first travelled around a little longer, enjoying the untramelled benefit of the money her mother had left to her.

She dismissed Malcolm's friends as 'poor sports'. Indeed, the only person of her acquaintance whom she classed as a 'good sport' was a young man named Lloyd Bradbury, whom she had first met in his capacity as second cashier to the Kentish County Bank at Sevenoaks. After her third visit, they had reached a stage of familiarity which seemed to warrant her inviting him over to Dorkham for the evening—she made sure it would be a Wednesday, when Malcolm always spent the evening at the golf club. Young Bradbury had always belonged to that class of bank

clerks who mix with their social superiors at all costs—which accounts for the fact that every member of the Big Five banks average a case a day of embezzlement.

Bradbury considered himself in clover at 'Three Gables', Dorkham. Not only was his hostess a very personable and charming young woman, not averse to what he described as 'a bit of fun', but there was also a selection of free drinks, which delighted his heart and considerably relieved his pocket, for most of his spare money found its way into hotel tills.

After his second visit, Frieda casually included him in a small party she was giving, and he met her husband, and considered him a very pleasant young man, and thought very little more about him at the time. He made no comment when he frequently returned home to find Bradbury sprawled in his favourite armchair, or occupying the hard court with Frieda. They had been married four years now, and he had an ever-growing connection to keep him occupied: in fact, there was some talk between himself and his cousin of buying up a firm in Frome which had discreetly approached them through a third party. Yes, Malcolm certainly had plenty to keep his mind occupied. And he always boasted that he and Frieda trusted each other.

That the affair between Lloyd Bradbury and Frieda Sutcliffe was the topic of a hundred tea tables in and around Sevenoaks would appear to have escaped him, and it might well have gently fizzled out as had so many of Frieda's early romances. But for the first time in her life, Frieda discovered that she was in love, at least as far as her shallow nature was capable of any such emotion. And Lloyd Bradbury was so highly infatuated with her that he too concluded it must be 'the real thing'.

Even now, all would have been well if they had maintained a bare minimum of discretion. But they seemed proud of their attachment; flaunted it defiantly beneath the noses of the county matrons and local squires. Naturally the latter considered it their duty to acquaint Malcolm Sutcliffe, who was generally liked, with the current state of affairs. One or two of them even

spoke to Lloyd Bradbury's manager, who summoned the young cashier to his office and laid down the law in no uncertain fashion. But Bradbury paid no heed; he knew the bank had no real jurisdiction over his leisure hours, as long as he did his job capably.

When Sutcliffe taxed Frieda on the subject, she was downright defiant, refused to give up Bradbury, and when her husband declared that he would forbid him to enter the house, retorted that she would then be under the necessity of visiting Bradbury—at his flat in Sevenoaks.

"Very well," said Malcolm quietly. "I won't forbid him the house. We'll simply leave the district. Then you'll soon get over this infatuation."

She could hardly believe her ears.

"Malcolm—what do you mean? How can we leave the district?" she gasped incredulously.

"I shall go and supervise the new branch at Frome," he told her.

"Then I shall stay here."

"Oh no, you won't. I propose to let this house furnished," he announced with a quiet decision that amazed her.

"I'll stay by myself in the district," she retorted.

He shook his head.

"I don't think so, because, you see, under those circumstances I couldn't make you any allowance."

She knew she was defeated. Her mother's income had stopped at her death, and the few hundreds she had left to Frieda had somehow slipped away in the intervening years.

"But Malcolm—" she began to protest.

"There's nothing more to be said," he replied coldly, and went across to the telephone.

"What are you going to do?" she asked in some trepidation.

"Telephone Roger Ludlow and put the house in his hands right away."

She turned and rushed from then room in a blazing fury, ran upstairs, and flung herself on the bed, sobbing hysterically.

* * * * * * *

A week later, Doctor Morelle and Miss Frayle were sitting in Roger Ludlow's office. He was looking for a country house on a short lease to enable him to enjoy a change of air, and also to conduct a certain amount of chemical research without any intrusion. He had always liked the wooded slopes and fertile valleys of this part of Kent, and it seemed that many others shared this preference.

"I'm afraid I have only one suitable residence on the books," sighed the agent, a pudgy young man, who looked ten years older than his actual age. "And that's only just come onto the market—it'll soon be snapped up too. I know it pretty well; the owner's quite a friend of mine. Lovely position—stands well on a hill—see for miles—every convenience, four good rooms downstairs—five bedrooms—two bathrooms—"

He paused to take a breath and handed over a photograph.

"Here you are, Doctor. Take a look at this picture."

"H'm...," murmured the Doctor, "Not unprepossessing in appearance. Is it possible to obtain possession in the near future?"

"Within the next few weeks. The owner is moving to Frome temporarily—but he tells me he expects to return possibly in about six months time. That is why there's only a short lease available."

"That would suit me admirably," agreed the Doctor, passing on the photograph to Miss Frayle.

"You'll find it well worth the trouble of inspection," Ludlow assured them. "In fact, it's liable to be snapped up any time."

"Yes, do let's go and see it, Doctor," put in Miss Frayle rather too eagerly for his liking.

"The owner will permit you to view any time you wish—within reason, of course," Ludlow informed them.

"I do not propose to inspect the property in the middle of the night," replied Doctor Morelle with a wintry smile.

"Quite," agreed Ludlow hurriedly. "I'm sure you'll find it

quite ideal for your purpose if you allow me to make an appointment."

"Can't we go along now?" demanded the persistent Miss Frayle. "It would save us another journey down here,"

The Doctor agreed with her for once.

"If you will excuse me a moment," said the agent, "I'll telephone the house, just to make sure either Mr. or Mrs. Sutcliffe is at home, and let them know we're coming along. It'll only take us about twenty minutes in the car—extremely convenient for shopping, you see...."

When they reached 'Three Gables', about half-an-hour later, a well-built young man with dark, wavy hair and heavy features was just coming out of the front door. He entered his rather battered saloon car and drove away without acknowledging their arrival, so the Doctor presumed that he could not be the owner of the house.

The Doctor observed that Ludlow's reaction to the young man's presence was a tiny frown, and then an expression of blank indifference.

They climbed out of the car, and entered the neat brick porch with its heavily studded front door. Ludlow rang the bell, and the door was opened almost at once by a striking young woman whom he addressed as Mrs. Sutcliffe.

She appeared to be quite pleased to see them, called Mr. Ludlow by his Christian name, and invited them inside.

"I'm so sorry my husband isn't here," she apologised. "He went out to see a friend just before you telephoned."

"I explained to Doctor Morelle and Miss Frayle," said Ludlow. "However, Mrs. Sutcliffe, no doubt you would be able to conduct us over the house."

"It's awfully attractive—and the garden's really lovely," supplemented Miss Frayle.

"I am glad you like it," smiled Mrs. Sutcliffe. "We've spent quite a lot of money there." She led the way out of the neatly panelled entrance hall through an archway.

"This is a sort of lounge," she began, moving across towards

the French windows. "We generally have our meals in this recess. There's a serving-hatch to the kitchen."

"That's very useful," commented Miss Frayle.

They made an exhaustive tour of the house, which was substantially built, well-decorated; and if some of the modern furniture had rather an uncomfortable aspect, the Doctor had to admit himself impressed by the general layout of the house. Miss Frayle was frankly enthusiastic.

"Thank you so much for showing us this beautiful home of yours," she said politely when the tour was complete.

"Yes, we're very grateful," added Ludlow, a little breathless from climbing stairs. "Pity Malcolm isn't here...."

"I can't think where he's got to—he should be back any minute," she replied.

"Perhaps if we walked around the grounds and surveyed the three acres you advertise," suggested the Doctor, "your husband will have returned by then."

"Yes—yes, of course," she agreed. "Roger, would you mind taking Doctor Morelle and Miss Frayle over the grounds and the paddock? I have rather an urgent phone call to make—I'll join you presently."

"Certainly, Mrs. Sutcliffe," agreed Ludlow with alacrity.

"You can go out this way." She opened the French windows for them.

When they were outside, Doctor Morelle turned to Ludlow, and asked:

"There is a garage, I presume?"

"Of course—jolly good garage—I've left my car in there several times. Room for three cars if they're not too big. This way...."

They approached the front doors of the garage. Ludlow went to open them, but they were locked.

"That's queer," he mused. "Malcolm doesn't generally lock them up when he's out with the car,"

"Perhaps he didn't take the car," suggested Miss Frayle.

Ludlow pushed his hat to the back of his head.

"From what I remember," he said thoughtfully, "the back doors are usually only on a catch...they're in two sections, and the top half comes open easily."

They went round to the rear, and the agent began pulling at the top half of the doors. Almost immediately, they noticed a strong smell of petrol fumes, and as the doors opened a wave of exhaust gas swept towards them.

"Stand back a moment!" ordered the Doctor, covering his face with his handkerchief.

"Whatever can have happened?" coughed Miss Frayle.

They could see now that there was a car in the garage.

"Somebody must have left the engine running," spluttered Ludlow. "It's Malcolm's car.... I thought he'd taken it...."

"The engine was left running for a very definite purpose," announced Doctor Morelle grimly indicating a man's form slumped over the wheel. It was the form of a slim man in his thirties, a slight tonsure showing as his head pitched forward.

"My God! It's Malcolm Sutcliffe!" gasped the agent, clasping the back of the car for support.

By a supreme effort of will, Miss Frayle choked back a scream.

"What a ghastly sight!" whispered the agent, his pudgy features assuming a bluish tinge. He grasped ineffectively at the smooth back of the saloon, then sank slowly to the ground.

"Doctor Morelle, he's fainted!" cried Miss Frayle.

"So I observe," said the Doctor in some astonishment. "It is usually *your* prerogative, Miss Frayle."

"I—I don't feel very well," she admitted, in what he imagined sounded rather a hopeful tone.

"Pull yourself together, Miss Frayle. This is not the first time in your life that you have been confronted by a body or bodies. Let us examine this one in the car...."

The air had cleared considerably now, and he was able to remove his handkerchief and bend over the inert form of Malcolm Sutcliffe.

"H'm...a case of carbon monoxide asphyxiation," he

announced after a very brief examination.

"Poor man," whispered Miss Frayle. "I suppose it must have been an accident."

He looked up, somewhat surprised. "Ah, Miss Frayle, I had taken it for granted that you had assumed your customary horizontal posture by this time."

"I'm feeling better," declared Miss Frayle defiantly.

"The Kentish air must agree with you. I wonder how much petrol is left in this tank?"

"Doesn't the gauge there show?" she asked.

"That indicates zero—because the engine has stopped."

"Shall I have a look in the tank?" she offered.

"Yes, I've no doubt you could see with the aid of a lighted match."

"Isn't that rather dangerous?" she demanded innocently.

"Remain where you are. I will ascertain the amount of petrol remaining by switching on the engine. The gauge will react accordingly."

He turned to the dashboard, only to find the ignition key missing. He searched the pigeonholes and the pockets of the car without success, then produced the key to his own car.

"Doubtless, this will fit," he murmured.

The engine spluttered into life, ran for a moment, then choked to a standstill.

"Is it all right, Doctor?" Miss Frayle asked.

"Perfectly. The petrol supply has not been exhausted—nearly two gallons remain."

Doctor Morelle withdrew the key, replaced it in his pocket, and crossed swiftly to where Roger Ludlow lay in an awkward position. Quickly, he loosened his collar.

The agent moaned.

"What happened?" he whispered, slowly recovering consciousness. Then he seemed to recall everything, and groaned again.

"Poor man," said Miss Frayle. "Perhaps if I got some water...."

"I took the liberty of extracting this brandy flask from the

car," said the Doctor. "He will probably need it when I impart a certain piece of information. The shock may be considerable."

"Another shock?" queried Miss Frayle in a puzzled voice.

"When I inform him that Mr. Sutcliffe has been murdered," declared the Doctor deliberately.

"Murdered!" gasped Miss Frayle. "Oh, Doctor...oh...."

There was a moan and a slight thud as she subsided against the garage wall.

"Stupid, incalculable young woman," snapped Doctor Morelle testily. "Why on earth should she want to faint now?"

* * * * * * *

They drove back to Sevenoaks, after breaking the news to Mrs. Sutcliffe, who reacted even more violently than they had anticipated. She screamed, shook her husband's inert form, fainted, recovered, screamed again, and relapsed into hysterics. It had taken them the better part of an hour to restore her. Roger Ludlow, sitting beside the Doctor, who was driving, seemed badly shaken by his experiences of the afternoon, and Miss Frayle in the back seat was rather white, and still clung to the small bottle of smelling-salts she always carried round in her bag.

"You didn't tell Mrs. Sutcliffe her husband was murdered," said Roger Ludlow at length.

"There seemed to be no point in arousing her to further histrionic display," replied the Doctor acidly.

The agent eyed him incredulously.

"You—you don't think she had anything to do with it?" he stammered.

The Doctor kept his eyes on the road ahead.

"At the moment, I prefer to make no conjecture until I have laid certain facts before the police," he answered. They hardly spoke again until the car drew up outside the police station. After they had each made a brief deposition. Doctor Morelle went into conference with the Inspector in charge.

"I still can't think how you can make such a rash statement," said Miss Frayle pensively, as they drove back to London.

"To what are you referring?"

"Saying that poor man was murdered. You had no real evidence."

"On the contrary," he snapped, "there was most conclusive evidence. The car was not of unusual manufacture, and the engine must have been started by an ignition key. That key was missing, however, and in order to test the petrol gauge by starting the car, I had to use my own. This was conclusive proof that someone had, after running the engine. returned subsequently and removed the key which he had used for the purpose."

"Well, yes, perhaps you're right...," she conceded with some reluctance. Then her face lit up. "Doctor...that young man who was leaving the house...it looked very much the same sort of car...."

"I have already notified the police to that effect," he calmly informed her. "At this moment, he is undergoing an intensive cross-examination. The Inspector told me there is a certain association between this young man and Mrs. Sutcliffe, so he will, doubtless, not have far to seek for a motive."

"It's all very regrettable," sighed the Doctor, after a further pause.

"Then you're sorry for her? I thought she was attractive, too."

"I am referring to our failure to conclude negotiations for the lease of the house," he retorted bitingly.

"But the place may be on the market—she wouldn't want to stay there now," she said brightening. "Even if she's proved innocent...."

He turned and swept her with a pitying glance.

"My dear Miss Frayle, you do not appear to appreciate that this trial will probably prove as highly sensational as any since that of Doctor Crippen. The house we have just seen will be a mecca for trippers from all over England. Perhaps you would

welcome the opportunity to show them round at a shilling a head!"

She subsided and said no more until they reached the outskirts of London. Then she sighed.

"I'm rather glad we're not going to live there after all." she told him.

"And why, pray?"

"Because," explained Miss Frayle with a shiver, "the house is almost certain to be haunted!"

THE CASE OF THE
INSURED JEWELS

It was natural, as a result of the great reputation that he had acquired, that Doctor Morelle should from time to time be called to attend to the great and the famous, in all walks of life. Miss Frayle sometimes regretted that she had not, when starting her work with the Doctor some years earlier, brought with her an autograph book in which, with care, she could have amassed a collection of signatures which would have been unique in the history of autographs, and which, at the same time, would have been extremely valuable. Famous writers, scientists, and artists came along with an almost monotonous regularity; film stars, from the great Carol James downwards, were almost weekly visitors to the Doctor's unpretentious house; and leaders in politics and industry, though not so frequent as those in the artistic professions, often called to see the Doctor on some obscure nervous disorder. There were occasions, also, on which princes and princesses came along—for it was but rarely that the Doctor could be persuaded to go and see them unless he was assured that it was a matter of life and death or that one of his beloved criminological problems were involved.

Yet to Miss Frayle, with her sympathetic outlook on the problems of suffering humanity, nothing was more interesting than the procession of diverse human beings which made its way, day by day, through the consulting room. She thought that they were really fascinating in their diversity.

One of the most fascinating women that the Doctor had

ever attended, Miss Frayle thought, was Mrs. Halsted, whose husband was by way of being an important person in business circles in the city of London—to wit, managing director of the Blue Star Insurance Company. She had been suffering from a nervous disorder which had baffled many doctors who were supposed to be expert in such matters. Yet Doctor Morelle had succeeded in diagnosing it, and, without much difficulty (so it appeared to Miss Frayle), had brought about a cure so surprising that to the sufferer and her husband it seemed to be something almost miraculous. The Doctor's account of the matter in the *Lancet*, which appeared some months later, was destined to become almost a classic in the annals of nervous disease.

It was therefore with some surprise that the Doctor, who was very busy dictating to Muss Frayle one morning a few weeks after the successful determination of Mrs. Halsted's illness, found that Mr. Halsted was waiting to see him.

When Halsted came in, Doctor Morelle looked at him with some curiosity. He thought that there was a definite appearance of anxiety in the man's eyes, and he at once offered Halsted a seat and waited for some revelation as to the reason why he was once more being consulted.

"It's very good of you to see me again, Doctor Morelle," Halsted said. "I often read of your activities, and I know of your very extensive practice, so I know what an extremely busy man you must be."

Miss Frayle looked at the man with human interest and sympathy. Her eyes had tears in them as she recalled the mental state in which Mrs. Halsted had recently been.

"I hope that your wife is getting on all right now, Mr. Halsted," she said.

Halsted smiled a rather wan smile. "Thank you, Miss Frayle," he replied, and then corrected himself. "Or rather, thanks to Doctor Morelle here," he added, "she's doing fine. There's no trace of any return of the old trouble."

Doctor Morelle had been studying the man with care while this conversation was going on. Now he said: "You yourself do

not appear to be in any need of *medical* attention, Mr. Halsted. Skin clear, hand steady, eyes a little strained perhaps...." He paused and turned to his amanuensis. "Ah, yes," he exclaimed with the air of a man who has made a great discovery. "Miss Frayle?"

Miss Frayle woke out of the daydream into which Halsted's remarks about his wife had plunged her. "Yes. Doctor," she said in her absent-minded manner.

"Take some notes. if you can regain your normal composure sufficiently to undertake any such mundane activity." There was a clear-cut air of decision about the Doctor's manner, which at once told Miss Frayle that he had come to a definite conclusion with regard to the reason why Halsted had decided to visit the consulting room on this morning.

"Notes, Doctor?" Miss Frayle said, in simulated surprise. "Notes about what?"

"Notes about the matter which Mr. Halsted wishes to discuss with us,"

"And that is...?" Miss Frayle was unable to give the Doctor the opportunity of showing off his brilliance of deduction in such a matter.

"I have no doubt that he is about to ask my advice with regard to the fate of some valuable jewellery which was lost, in somewhat mysterious circumstances, a week ago," the Doctor said with a smile of triumph that might almost be described as a smirk, if the Doctor had not been too dignified a person ever to indulge in that extremely undignified gesture.

Halsted looked at the Doctor in the most complete amazement. His eyes gaped, his mouth opened wide. There was something almost comic about his surprise,

"Great Scott, Doctor!" he exclaimed. "How on earth did you guess what I...?"

"As I recall it," Doctor Morelle went on, "the individual who apparently mislaid the gems is named Helen Blane, a professional actress."

If Halsted had been surprised before, he was now practically

speechless with amazement, He managed to gasp out the words: "This is amazing!"

Miss Frayle was equally impressed. She had, in her tine with Doctor Morelle, seen many extraordinarily impressive examples of his almost uncanny mental powers; but this was perhaps the most impressive of them all.

"How have you managed to guess it, Doctor Morelle?" she asked, her eyes wide open with astonishment,

There was a sneering tone in the Doctor's voice as he replied: "My dear Miss Frayle," he said, "you have surely been in association with me long enough now to know that I never indulge in that pernicious habit known as guessing, When I am faced with a problem, no matter how difficult it may appear to be on the surface, I do not guess; I deduce."

Halsted still looked surprised, however. "Not a soul, I thought, knew that I was coming to consult you about the disappearance of those jewels," he said.

Doctor Morelle took a deep breath, as if he was containing himself with great difficulty. Then he went on, explaining with an attitude of restraint: "You have informed us that your wife is still in perfect health. I can easily see for myself that you are reasonably well, though possibly a little overanxious about something as yet undisclosed by you. Therefore, it is obvious that it is not any medical matter about which you have approached me."

"That's true enough," Halsted agreed.

"And, since I have in recent years acquired what I may describe, I think, as a considerable reputation in dealing with criminological matters, I may take it that it is in some way in connection with a crime that you wish to consult me."

Halsted looked not altogether convinced by this analysis of the position.

"But I still don't quite see how you decided that it was in connection with the jewels of Miss Blane that I wanted to see you, Doctor," he argued.

Doctor Morelle smiled. "It is surely obvious enough," he

said. "You are managing director of a large and important insurance company. I noticed in the Press last week a report of the loss of the precious stones in question. I assume that the insurance company concerned—your own—will have to pay a considerable sum in settlement of the claim, Naturally, if there is any doubt about the way in which the stones disappeared, you will want to have the matter investigated by one who may be described as an expert in crime—which, I suggest, is a description which can not unfairly be applied to myself."

Halsted laughed. "Pretty good, Doctor," he said, "Your deductions are, of course, absolutely correct."

"I must say, Doctor Morelle," Miss Frayle added, her eyes fairly glowing with excitement and admiration for her employer, "that really is most awfully smart of you!"

"Thank you, my dear Miss Frayle," replied the Doctor with a slight bow. But there was an undercurrent of sarcasm in his voice that she did not altogether like,

Halsted's handsome face set, however, in an expression of grim determination, "But seriously, Doctor," he said, "this is a pretty important matter for me, And I need your help badly, I must admit. This time it is not on my wife's behalf, but on my own—or rather, my firm's."

Doctor Morelle nodded gravely. He realized readily enough that even the greatest insurance companies would not be ready to pay out a sum as great as that involved in this case unless the whole matter were submitted to the most stringent investigation.

"What precisely," the Doctor asked quietly, "is this actress person's status in her somewhat disreputable profession?"

"She's famous for her lovely red hair!" exclaimed Miss Frayle, without any apparent reason,

"I am not," Doctor Morelle pointed out, "enquiring after her pulchritudinous assets—if red hair of that particular type may justifiably be regarded as an asset."

"I think it may!" Miss Frayle exclaimed with an ecstatic smile. "In fact, I have often wondered whether it wouldn't be as

well for me to try...."

"Miss Frayle," snapped the Doctor, "kindly refrain from bringing your beauty parlour vanities into this discussion, which, I would remind. you, is concerned with the disappearance of some jewellery, and not with the alleged beauties of an actress."

Halsted had listened to this exchange of remarks with a smile, though his own feelings were serious enough, as he had already indicated.

"Miss Blane is a cabaret star," he explained, "although I must say, Doctor, that I think she could be better described as notorious than as famous."

Doctor Morelle's expression showed his distaste with cabaret stars. "Personally," he said, "I should describe all such seekers after the limelight and vulgar sensationalism as notorious rather than famous."

Miss Frayle smiled secretly to herself. "You are hardly a blushing violet yourself," she murmured, scarcely realizing that she had spoken her thoughts aloud.

"You said something, I think, Miss Frayle?" the Doctor said, rounding sharply on her.

"Nothing, nothing," Miss Frayle replied, regretting that she had allowed herself to speak aloud.

"I thought that I heard you make some remark about violets," Doctor Morelle pursued.

"I merely remarked that I was very fond of violets," Miss Frayle remarked, trying to get out of the awkward position in which her indiscreet words had landed her. She felt that the Doctor was still more than a trifle suspicious, although outwardly he showed no sign of having any knowledge of what she had actually said.

"A remark singularly inane, in that it has no connection with the matter which is at present under discussion," he said,

"I'm in a very awkward spot, Doctor Morelle, and I'm hoping that you will be able to do something to help," Halsted explained.

"What is the particular difficulty which faces you at the moment?" Doctor Morelle asked.

"I just can't call in the police to deal with this case," the man explained.

"Why not?"

"Well, it would be tantamount of accusing Miss Blane of some more or less criminal action. And if we failed to find anything wrong with her claim, it would lay us open to some considerable unpleasantness from our client."

"I understand," agreed Doctor Morelle.

"But, all the same, you think that she is up to something pretty fishy?" Miss Frayle said, thinking that it was time that she showed an intelligent interest in what was going on, if only to offset the unfortunate results of her remarks about violets, which the Doctor now appeared to have forgotten, but which, she was sure, were still at the back of his mind, to be produced at a convenient moment in the future.

Halsted considered with care before he replied to this question. Then he said: "We're not altogether happy about the purchase of her jewels in the first place."

Doctor Morelle's sense of logic was offended by the way in which these questions and answers were going on. "First of all," he said, "acquaint me with the circumstances under which the gems were lost, if you don't mind, Mr. Halsted. Is there any possible question of theft?"

"Oh no," Halsted said. "That has never been suggested, I think."

"Well, pray proceed with your account of what happened when the jewels were lost," Doctor Morelle said.

"The lady is the...er...." Halsted hesitated, and then took this hurdle with a jump. "She is the friend of a certain Baron Roselle," he said.

"A foreigner?" asked Miss Frayle, reacting as might be expected of her in the circumstances.

"Yes," Halsted agreed. "The couple were returning from the Continent, where they had been spending a few weeks' holiday.

They crossed by the boat from Dieppe. As they stood on deck, the Baron happened to bump into Miss Blane, who happened at that precise moment to be holding her jewel-case. As a result it was flung from her grasp, went overboard, and is at present at the bottom of the English Channel, somewhere between Dieppe and Newhaven. That, at any rate, is the lady's story of the accident, and I may say that she shows every sign of intending to stick to it."

"You don't believe it?" Doctor Morelle asked bluntly.

"The whole thing appears to have happened too conveniently," explained Halsted. "It is difficult for us to disprove; yet it seems to be such an obvious case for possible fraud that...." His voice trailed away uncertainly, as if he found it not at all easy to put his suspicions into precise words.

"Were there any witnesses to the alleged accident?" Doctor Morelle asked.

"Plenty," answered Halsted sadly. "Miss Blane and the Baron are able to call at least four passengers who definitely saw the jewel-case fall into the sea, There is no doubt about that, no doubt at all."

"And yet you suspect that some act of trickery has taken place?" Doctor Morelle pursued.

"Yes."

"H'm." It seemed, for the moment, that Doctor Morelle found the case puzzling even to his superlative analytical intellect. Then he went on: "You have told me that the—er—lady is in some respects notorious. Have you any reliable information concerning the precise status and ability of her—er—friend, the Baron Roselle?"

"You mean, Doctor, that you think he may be a phoney?" Miss Frayle asked in excited tones.

"Miss Frayle!" exclaimed the Doctor. "Your Americanisms are truly shocking to the sensitive ear."

"Oh," answered Halsted, "he is a genuine Baron all right. We have had various enquiries made into all that sort of thing. That was the obvious first line of attack."

"But you still retain certain, possibly ill-defined, suspicions of Miss Blane and the Baron?" Doctor Morelle insisted.

"Yes. You see, we have reason to suppose that they are both pretty hard-up."

"What caused their state of financial stringency?" Doctor Morelle asked.

"They have extravagant tastes, both of them," Halsted explained. "And, I should think that they have been living beyond their incomes for years past."

Doctor Morelle grinned grimly. "They would appear to be quite a delectable couple," he remarked.

"Helen Blane's awfully attractive," Miss Frayle mused with an air of envy.

"Beauty," Doctor Morelle snapped at her, "is only skin deep. That is a fact for which you, my dear Miss Frayle, should be duly grateful!"

Miss Frayle looked somewhat taken aback by this attack. "When it's too late," she murmured. "I expect that I'll think of a suitable answer to that one."

"What did the precious stones comprise?" Doctor Morelle enquired of Halsted, patiently ignoring Miss Frayle's sotto-voce remark.

"I've got a list of them here," Halsted said, producing a sheet of paper from his pocket.

"Good," Doctor Morelle commented. "Would you read it to me, please?"

Halsted read: "Diamond and sapphire bracelet, valued at £6,000, pair of ruby earrings, valued £5,000."

"Is that all?" Doctor Morelle asked.

Halsted smiled. "There are some smaller items, also an emerald necklace, valued at £10,000. The smaller items are of no real importance; but you will see that when three items total £19,000 the matter is a big thing, even for a company of the size of mine."

Doctor Morelle again mused, "Doubtless," he said, "you hold the receipts regarding the money which she had paid for those

three large items?"

Halsted agreed, "I've got the receipts with me," he said, "Why do you ask?"

"Might I have the opportunity of perusing them?" Doctor Morelle asked.

Again Halsted fumbled with papers in his pocket, and finally handed over the documents, "Here they are," he said. "They seem to be in order."

"But you have your doubts?"

"Yes,"

Doctor Morelle took the proffered receipts and examined them with considerable care. Miss Frayle noted that he spread them out on the desk, scanned them rapidly, and then appeared to be comparing the three receipts, as if he anticipated finding some contradictions between them. Miss Frayle was not at all sure what the Doctor expected to find; but she knew that he would inevitably lay his finger on the weak spot of the case, if such a weak spot did, in fact, exist.

"I perceive," Doctor Morelle remarked, "that the diamond and sapphire bracelet, the emerald necklace, and the ruby earrings were all purchased by the same firm, though at widely varying dates."

"Yes."

"Are you," the Doctor went on, "in any way acquainted with this firm?"

"Yes."

"Have they a good reputation in business circles?"

"Not bad. But it is practically a one-man business," explained Halsted.

"And who is the individual behind it?" Doctor Morelle asked. Miss Frayle, watching the Doctor's face, felt sure that he had already laid his finger on the vital clue which would soon reveal the solution of the mystery.

"A chap called Thomson," Halsted said. "Came to London from Edinburgh about fifteen years ago. He set up in Hatton Garden as a diamond merchant, and afterwards he opened a

retail shop in Bond Street—the shop where Miss Blane bought these jewels. I've had his business connections pretty closely investigated; it's said there's virtually nothing against him. If there is some sort of fraud involved in this affair, it will be the first time that anything of the kind has been alleged against him. I've been pretty discreet in my enquiries, but I think that I can safely say that nothing criminal has ever been brought home to him—or, for that matter, ever suspected."

"But in spite of that," persisted Doctor Morelle, "you still suspect this individual of being in some way implicated with this woman and her companion?"

Halsted hesitated before replying, as if he found the whole business infinitely distasteful. "Yes," he answered at length, "I suspect that there is something queer about the receipts. But without some sort of proof, I'm stuck. And my reason for coming to you is that I thought you might be able to do something in the way of supplying that proof."

Doctor Morelle looked at his secretary, "Miss Frayle!" he snapped sharply.

"Yes, Doctor?"

"Have your notebook handy, please, if you will be so kind."

"Certainly, Doctor." Miss Frayle was gently surprised at this request, but she always tried very hard not to reveal any kind of astonishment at whatever Doctor Morelle might show himself disposed to do. From long experience she knew only too well that the Doctor's actions, however incomprehensible they night appear to be on the surface, had a way of turning out in the end to be sensible and capable of leading to satisfactory results.

"Will you kindly note down the details of the receipts which Mr. Halsted has given me?"

"Certainly, Doctor Morelle." Miss Frayle had her pencil poised at the 'ready'.

"One diamond and sapphire bracelet," Doctor Morelle read, "purchased October 15, 1938."

Miss Frayle scribbled hurriedly, "One diamond and sapphire bracelet," she repeated slowly, "purchased October 15, 1938."

Doctor Morelle looked annoyed. "If you could possibly refrain from repeating it aloud after me!" he snapped. "Just content yourself with writing it down as accurately as possible, if you do not mind."

"Yes, Doctor Morelle," said Miss Frayle meekly. Halsted looked gently surprised at the quiet way in which she took this rebuke. But he did not know the long course of training that Miss Frayle had undergone in order to reach this state of meekness.

"Emerald necklace," Doctor Morelle went on, picking up the second receipt, "purchased July 23, 1943. Have you got that down, Miss Frayle?"

"Yes, Doctor."

"And finally," said the Doctor, "pair of ruby earrings, purchased December 18, 1946. Have you got all those details down, Miss Frayle?"

"Yes, Doctor, But...Dr. Morelle...." Miss Frayle was clearly seething with intense excitement, a state in which Doctor Morelle always disliked seeing her. He was wont to say that in such a condition Miss Frayle was the most impossible guide to logical thought which it was possible to imagine. And possibly he was right.

"A moment, Miss Frayle, please," he said, dismissing her excitement with a wave of the hand. "Mr. Halsted," he went on, turning to the insurance man, "you observe nothing wrong with those receipts?"

"They seem clear and above-board to me," Halsted admitted, wondering just what was the point to which the Doctor wished him to direct his attention.

"Are you certain about that?"

"Absolutely, The signature is Thomson's, all right. I've taken the trouble to have that investigated," explained Halsted. "I've compared those signatures with literally dozens of genuine signatures of the man, and there can, I think, be no doubt that these are absolutely genuine."

"Yes?" The rise in Doctor Morelle's eyebrows, and the

inflexion of his voice suggested that he was still not altogether satisfied by the insurance man's reaction to the questions that were being put to him.

"There's nothing odd about the three twopenny stamps, either," Halsted went on. "No, I can't for the life of me see that there is any chance of disputing the reality of those receipts. And if we can't dispute the reality of those receipts, I don't see that there is any chance at all of getting away with the case. It may be Miss Blane, the Baron, and Thomson are all in this together, but I fail to see what chance we have got of proving it. That, indeed, is why I came to you in the first instance, Doctor, hoping that you would be able to see a loophole where—quite frankly—I can see none at all."

Doctor Morelle smiled grimly. "Well, Mr. Halsted," he said, "in that case, I suppose it might be considered an advantageous stroke of policy to hear just what it is that Miss Frayle has so obviously been bursting to tell us for the past five minutes."

Miss Frayle, however, no longer appeared to be quite so anxious to dispense information as she had been a bit earlier. She hesitated and then muttered various things, which the Doctor found quite impossible to comprehend.

"Will you be so kind as to explain precisely what you are endeavouring to tell us, Miss Frayle?" he said in his most irritated tones.

"I've got a definite feeling, Doctor," Miss Frayle began, only to be almost immediately interrupted by her employer.

"I think," he said, "that we might leave your intuitive inspirations out of the case, Miss Frayle. All that I have asked you for and all that I require at the present juncture, is your opinion of the facts in front of you."

Miss Frayle smiled. "The facts don't seem to be at all in dispute, Doctor," she said.

"No?" There was an air of healthy scepticism about the Doctor's voice, which did not altogether escape Miss Frayle's attention, so that she felt that she must do her best to justify what she had been saying, and do it without in any way appearing to

be making more excuses.

"Well," she said. "I can't see that there is anything wrong with the receipts, of course."

"No?" Again there was that sceptical monosyllable, which Miss Frayle found so extremely irritating and at the same time almost menacing in its implications.

"No," she said. "Mr. Halsted has assured us that he has no doubt that the three signatures are genuine. The stamps are all right—they're all alike—and I can't see that anyone could suggest that there is anything in any way illegal or irregular about the three receipts."

"No?" Doctor Morelle queried for the third time. "Then in that case, my dear Miss Frayle, might I perhaps be so bold as to enquire precisely what important information it was that you were so keen to impart to us a few minutes ago when I was engaged in obtaining from Mr. Halsted facts which, in my own humble opinion, were more directly germane to the issue which we are at present trying to bring to a successful conclusion."

"My intuition," Miss Frayle said, albeit rather hesitatingly, "tells me that no woman with red hair could possibly...."

Doctor Morelle's face became furious with anger. "The colour of her hair, Miss Frayle," he snapped, "has nothing whatever to do with the case. On the other hand, there are facts that have to be borne in mind, and which undoubtedly point to...."

It was now Halsted's turn to interrupt. "Something tells me, Doctor," he said, "that you have some suspicions about the woman, all the same."

"I have no suspicions," Doctor Morelle said firmly.

"But, surely, Doctor," Miss Frayle said, and then, catching a glimpse of his expression, she came to a halt. It was unwise she knew, to 'bait' him too far. And she knew now that the point of explosion was not very far away.

"I did not suspect," the Doctor repeated. "When a case reaches the stage now reached in this one, I never suspect. I *know*."

"You know?" Halsted could scarcely believe his ears. "You

mean to say, Doctor Morelle, that you know what has been going on in this affair?"

Doctor Morelle nodded somewhat morosely. "Yes, Mr. Halsted," he said. "I know that this is a palpable conspiracy to defraud your firm, carried out by the three individuals whose names you mentioned earlier."

"You mean that, Doctor?" Halsted said.

"Mr. Halsted, I am not in the habit of making bland assertions which I cannot support by undoubted facts. I can assure you," the Doctor said, "that if you will communicate with the police you will not have to pay the thousands of pounds claimed by the lady in the case, but that the police will undoubtedly have the pleasure of a successful prosecution for fraud and conspiracy against the three people whose nefarious activities we have been discussing for the past half hour or so."

"Well," said Miss Frayle, "it would seem that the feminine intuition which you look at so scornfully, Doctor is not so far off the mark, after all."

Doctor Morelle's eyes flashed utter contempt. "My dear Miss Frayle," he said, "when the criminals are apprehended, which they will be as soon as Mr. Halsted has the opportunity of communicating with the police, it will be as the result of my own logical deduction, and not as the result of any brilliant strokes of intuition by yourself."

Miss Frayle smiled. "Of course, Doctor," she said, "I know that those people must have made some dreadful mistake which you were at once able to pounce upon like a cat on a mouse."

"I was not aware," commented Doctor Morelle icily, "that my characteristics were so notably feline."

"I'm so sorry, Doctor," apologised Miss Frayle, "but I think that you know what I mean."

"I know one thing, at any rate," the Doctor remarked.

"And that is?" Halsted said. The insurance man had listened to this exchange of compliments with some amusement; but he thought that it was time that the conversation was brought back to the right lines, since he was extremely anxious to know just

what had gone on, the method by which Doctor Morelle had arrived at the conclusion that a definite act of fraud had been carried out by the three conspirators.

"That is that Miss Frayle held the vital clue under her very nose, yet failed to appreciate its real significance, in spite of all that feminine intuition to which she appears to attach so much value and importance...."

"Well, I am a bit short-sighted, you know, Doctor," Miss Frayle retorted.

"Nonsense!" snapped the Doctor. "Even at this moment, I am sure that you have not the slightest idea of the clue to which I have been referring."

"That's true, I haven't," admitted Miss Frayle sadly.

"You observed clearly, in spite of your astigmatism, that the receipts were all in perfect order," the Doctor pointed out.

"Yes," Miss Frayle said. "The signatures and the stamps were exactly the same in the three cases."

"Precisely!" The Doctor glared round him with an air of positive triumph. "And that," he cackled, "is why I say that I know with absolute certainty that there was a conspiracy to defraud the insurance company on the part of the three individuals whose abilities and activities we have been discussing this morning."

"But I still don't see," Miss Frayle began, only once more to be interrupted by the Doctor.

"The stamps were exactly the same," he said. "That is the vital clue, Miss Frayle, the precise significance of which so curiously eluded you."

"But surely, Doctor," Mr. Halsted said, his brow wrinkled in bewilderment, "it would be anticipated that the stamps would be the same. Three twopenny stamps, all during the reign of our present king, would naturally be alike."

"The stamp dated October 15, 1938, would, in actual fact, have been a quite different shade from the other two," the Doctor pointed out calmly.

"Really, Doctor?" Miss Frayle said.

"Yes, Miss Frayle," explained the Doctor. "The shade of stamps was altered in 1941. That was a wartime measure, which was introduced, I understand, in order to save the dye which was in the ink. The receipt, dated 1938, should have borne a stamp of a much deeper orange colour than the two that bore later dates. In court, it would be totally impossible for any counsel to oppose that fact. It would be sufficient of itself to prove that the whole affair was based on forged receipts. And, when once that fact had been established, the whole case is naturally worked out to an inexorable and completely logical conclusion."

"That's brilliant, Doctor," Halsted said. "I'm sure that my directors will be immensely obliged to you for so neatly putting your finger on the really crucial clue in this very difficult affair."

For once, however, Miss Frayle proved to be irrepressible.

"Of course, Doctor," she said, "you spotted a very important point."

"That is extremely kind of you, Miss Frayle," he said with a sarcastic smile. "It is good for you to let me know that what I do meets with your unqualified approval."

"But I still think," she went on, "that my clue, actually, was just as good as yours; and it was one which you didn't mention, and which it is just possible you didn't notice."

Doctor Morelle's voice took on a harsher tone than usual. "I can hardly contain my impatience to hear this marvellous clue which you have hit upon, no doubt with the aid of your celebrated intuition, Miss Frayle," he said.

"No woman with flaming red hair would spend thousands of pounds to buy a pair of ruby earrings," Miss Frayle explained. "I mean to say, think of the clash of colour. Think of how dreadful they would look against her hair."

For once Miss Frayle had the unaccustomed pleasure of seeing Doctor Morelle completely taken aback, "Well, I...I...," he stuttered. "That is to say, that I...I...."

And Miss Frayle could not resist her little moment of complete triumph. "Yes, Doctor," she said, "you know, you did miss that clue altogether! And I do believe that you're going slightly ruby

red in the face yourself!"

ABOUT THE AUTHOR
(1908-2006)

by Philip Harbottle

Born in July 1908 in Dudley, Worcestershire as Vivian Ernest Coltman-Allen, Ernest Dudley grew up in Cookham, Berkshire, where his father kept a hotel. Stanley Spencer lived next door, and was a friend of the family. Through Spencer's patrons, the hotel became a meeting place for artists and actors. Ivor Novello was a weekend fixture. The comedian and film star Jack Buchanan helped the young Ernest rehearse a song for an amateur concert.

At the age of seventeen Ernest left boarding school and joined a theatre company touring Shakespeare through provincial Ireland, in village halls and cowsheds. From this he graduated to the more upscale Charles Doran Company, and performed in proper theatres, paying its actors the munificent sum of £2 a week. For the rest of life he used and was known by his stage name of Ernest Dudley

Always one with an eye for the ladies, Ernest soon met and teamed up with his late wife, the celebrated actress Jane Grahame.

Jane came from a theatrical family: her stepfather was Ellie Norwood, famous silent film actor who played Sherlock Holmes on stage. Through these family connections, Ernest secured work in the West End, appearing with Charles Laughton and Fay Compton, amongst others. When the original production

of Noel Coward's *PRIVATE LIVES* transferred to Broadway, it was he and his wife who were recruited to take over the Laurence Olivier and Gertrude Lawrence roles in the British touring production.

His wife regularly played leading roles in the stage plays of Edgar Wallace, and Ernest would later create for her the character of Miss Frayle, assistant to Dr. Morelle in his radio plays. Other actresses would later take over the role. Most notably Sylvia Sims. Amongst the actors who played the good Doctor was Cecil Parker.

In the 1930s and 1940s he worked regularly for the BBC. In July 1942 his famous detective character (modelled on the autocratic film actor Eric von Stronheim, who he had met in Paris in the 1930s) 'Dr. Morelle' made his radio debut on *MONDAY NIGHT AT EIGHT*. Dr. Morelle was a big hit with listeners, and engendered a long cycle of novels and short stories, a play and a film, and three series on radio. At around the same time, he launched another very successful radio programme, *THE ARMCHAIR DETECTIVE*, which ran for many years, and Ernest became known as "The BBC Armchair Detective." In this weekly programme he reviewed the best of the current releases of detective novels, dramatising a chapter from each. They included his dramatization of John Russell Fearn's 1947 novel *ONE REMAINED SEATED*, and it was this fact that would cause Fearn's biographer Philip Harbottle to seek Dudley out some fifty years later, to become his friend and agent. Notable amongst his many other radio credits is the fact that he was the first-ever radio jazz critic. In the 1950s he transferred to BBC television with an early audience participation programme, *Judge for Yourself.*

Back in the 1930s Ernest also ran a parallel career as a newspaper journalist, specialising and pioneering in show business gossip, working for a time with Val Guest, with whom he had also earlier worked as a film scriptwriter in the British "quota" studio system. Amongst his many newspaper 'scoops' was how he had collaborated with actor Fred Astaire in a London night-

club on the creation of a new dance-step.

All of which only gives the bare bones of an amazing career as, variously, an actor, sports correspondent, jazz critic, playwright, novelist, gossip columnist, screenwriter and crime reporter. Most amazing is the fact that he became a marathon runner at an age when other people were drawing their pensions and relaxing by the fireside, and competed in several New York Marathons, writing a best selling book on how he achieved his amazing feats, *RUN FOR YOUR LIFE*.

Apart from some fourteen Dr. Morelle books, Ernest also published during his lifetime a dozen other detective novels, mostly notably *THE HARASSED HERO* (1951) which was subsequently filmed. He also appeared with short stories in leading detective periodicals such as *John Creasey Mystery Magazine* and, in the U.S.A., *Ellery Queen Mystery Magazine*. In the 1960s, and the following decades, he became established as the author of a long series of "animal" books for children, including *RANGI*, the story of a Highland rescue dog, and *RUFUS: THE STORY OF A FOX*. Ernest has also written novelisations of a number of films, along with a range of best-selling non-fiction books on diverse subjects, most notably *CHANCE AND THE FIRE HORSES* (Harvill Press, 1972) bringing to life Victorian London and telling the story of a dog, famous at the time, called Chance, who became attached to the fire brigade, and a favourite of the Prince of Wales.

An expert and enthusiast on the exploits of Sherlock Holmes because of his wife's family connections, Ernest wrote a two-act stage play, *THE RETURN OF SHERLOCK HOLMES*, which was successfully staged and taken on tour in 1993, with Michael Cashman as Holmes.

In 2002 a US publisher, Wildside Press, began to reprint some of his best detective novels, including a number of 'Dr. Morelle' adventures, in print on demand paperback format, available online. In 2005, the leading English publishers of 'large print' editions, F. A. Thorpe, began featuring Ernest's detective novels, in their Linford Mystery series, including the

'Dr. Morelle' books. All fourteen Morelle titles were quickly reprinted, followed by a number of new posthumous short story collections compiled by his friend and agent Philip Harbottle. These contained several unpublished Morelle short stories discovered in the author's effects, plus novelizations of radio and stage scripts.

Ernest continued writing right up to the end of his life. His last novelette, 'The Beetle', featuring Edgar Allan Poe's famous detective Auguste Dupin, was based on an earlier play broadcast on BBC radio, entitled *The Flies of Isis*. The new story was accepted for a Canadian anthology of Poe's 'Dupin' stories, alongside pastiche stories by John Dickson Carr and Charles Dickens. Ernest was checking the proofs in hospital at the time of his death. The anthology was fated not to appear, but 'The Beetle' has now been included in his new posthumous detective story collection, *DEPARTMENT OF SPOOKS*.

He is survived by his only daughter, Susan Dudley-Allen, a resident of New York in the U.S.A., who is devotedly overseeing the restoration of an amazing literary career.